I0456609

THE
ONLY HOUSE

A NOVEL BY
ED WOOD

FOR ENTERTAINMENT OF ADULTS

Encyclopocalypse Publications
www.encyclopocalypse.com

The Only House by Edward D. Wood Jr.
Originally published: June 7, 1972

This edition, build and design Copyright © 2024 by Severin Films
and Encyclopocalypse Publications
All rights reserved.

First Edition
ISBN: 978-1-960721-88-4

Cover artwork by David Levine
Cover layout and design by Amy Voorhees Searles and Gary Herz
Interior design and formatting by Mark Alan Miller and Sean
Duregger
Edited by Mark Alan Miller

THE
ONLY HOUSE

1

THEY WERE THE CARPENTERS, and they were extremely unhappy...a state of mind which had existed for the entire six months they had been married. It was a strong un-happiness which threatened at every moment to pull them apart, explode the very world which both had looked so longingly toward, through the illusion of rose colored glasses.

All her young life Shirley had been brought up in a home of puritan values, determination and point of view. Sex was spoken of, but in pure moralistic values and never in front of her. It was something she heard behind solid oak doors. But the girl was taught thoroughly that her virginity was to be saved for her future husband. Her body must never be defiled before that time of the marriage vows.

Shirley conquered her fears long before she conquered her conscience. Then again perhaps she never did fully conquer that strong, deep-seated conscience. Her parents had instilled their right and wrong, and the fears of the punishment of God into her from the time she was old enough to realize what was being said. And those thoughts and demands were retained throughout the formative years of grade school and even into the first years of high school. But there the changes began to take place, All the fears which were implanted deep within her mind caused her to think more readily and more thoroughly than most of her other classmates.

But there were the words, sentences, ideas and ideals which drifted to her eager ears. They were completely different, strange, much stronger in context than those which she had learned and listened to at home. At home it was like entering a different world entirely...a world completely drawn within itself, with its own mental and moral standards, those directed by her father; a narrow minded bigot. Leaving the house, or entering it, was the complete slamming of a door. It represented two completely different lifetimes.

For the longest while she fought against those outside elements...entities...rejected the very thought that there really was something other than the teachings of her father...that others outside of his house might have different ideas than those she had learned. But there were thousands of people in the outside world, and there were only the two back at her father's house who directed her...her mother and her father...all important, her father.

The *numbers* (by reason of simply *that*) the numbers had to win out. There was no fighting against the odds. And in her own deep thinking mind she knew it would be with the outside world where she would have to spend the rest of her life. Her father and her mother and their house necessarily had to grow old and go soon into decay. She had to force open her mind to the outside world. And the outside world was one of sex, utter pure sex in all its tremendous scope. But sex was a word never spoken in her presence in her father's house. He furthered that it meant everything which was vile, dirty, filthy, monstrous in the world. The reason for all the corruption and degeneracy in the world.

That was what she had been told when the word came up that one and only time. The first and last time. And the tirade her father spewed upon hearing it pronounced from Shirley's youthful, eager glowing lips caused her to never use it in his, or her mother's, presence ever again.

But that word among other words which were characteristic of that mother word were ever-present outside the house. The relating words were sometimes said boisterously, laughingly, tauntingly, then at other times, softly, sensuously, seriously. Whatever tone, whatever inflection was used the words took on new connotations. The inflections held all the meaning behind their delivery. She didn't have to possess very intense thoughts to understand any of their meanings once she had learned the words.

However, as with all the young, or at least most of the young, words soon were not enough for complete explanations. Words had to have some feeling attached the them. This especially was directed to the off color words such as she had learned outside of school. They were all sexually directed, oriented, designed, planted. And sex was supposed to be the greatest feeling, sensation of all.

Tommy Kemper was to be her teacher where those feelings, those sensations were concerned. And the classroom was to be a small grassy knoll behind thick bushes beyond the school yard. And the period of learning time was to be just after dark in a session whereby she could easily explain her lateness to her father.

She remained after school. She often did on Wednesday. It was a special sewing class and there would never be a checking up on her when it came to accomplish the bright arts of sewing, knitting or crocheting...all the puritan virtues of the homebody.

Tommy Kemper didn't have to plead very hard. Just enough so he could say she didn't give in easily. She had heard what the boys said when a girl gave in easy, was a push-over. But she had to find out what it was all about so she certainly didn't want to frighten the boy away with a bunch of parry or thrusts. She couldn't resist his preliminary advances too strongly. The girls had said it was the thing to do if she wanted to be in with the crowd. And it had to be with Tommy Kemper. She liked him best of all the other boys. it would be best to do it with him. And everybody, even mothers and fathers were doing that sort of thing all the time. So if mothers and fathers were doing it, then it was alright. It was only priests and nuns who didn't do such things. But who were they! They didn't know much about anything outside of their own houses either, just like her father's house.

She'd heard the names for those intimate parts of a boy's body. She'd also heard all the names, medical as well as crude about a girl's body...but all she had to do was look into a mirror, in the privacy of her own room. She felt her room wasn't really a part of her father's house. It was her domain. There she fixed the names to her body parts. But it would not be so easy to put the names to the parts of a boy's body. And she didn't want to act like a complete dummy. She just couldn't come right out and ask Tommy Kemper what this was or what that was and what was that hose-like thing...but that one she could guess. The girls had described something like that so she guessed what word affixed itself to that thing. But she couldn't understand what allthe fuss was about in such a hose-like piece of flesh and muscle. And the things that hung down under it with all the hair...a really ugly something...they looked like over weighted, sagging water bags...stretched beyond redemption.

She didn't like the sight right from the start. She didn't like it any better when it was no longer just sticking out through the front of Tommy's trousers and it was completely naked hanging there between his hairless legs. And she liked it even less when it stood straight out next to her when he and she lay side by side on the grass. The thing appeared to be throbbing and there was a purple knob on the end and that seemed to be making some kind of a sucking noise"

But that was all her imagination!

She didn't mind his hands slipping up through the legs of her new pink panties and pulling them down the length of her legs after having lifted her skirt. Nylon always felt good: a soft feeling that she'd always enjoyed and many times when she had gone to the toilet and when finished, she slipped the panties up and down several times before continuing on with her other business simply because she did like the feeling of the material sliding up and down.

And she liked the feeling of the cool grass on her naked thighs and later on her rump. She had lain naked other times when there was no one around, when she was out in the woods on a hike or something. She even felt comfortable as his fingers neatly unbuttoned the front of her green angora cardigan and he dipped into her brassiere to free the youthful mounds which still had some distance to grow.

His hands were warm, but so was the weather. Earlier she wished she had worn simply a blouse instead of the angora sweater because the afternoon had been stiflingly hot. But it had cooled off and she knew it would cool off even more as the darkness settled. Perhaps the Angora sweater had been the right choice after all. And she felt the breeze capture her naked breasts as his hands left one for the other, then returned back to the first again. Then she felt his lips caressing the nipple and his lips found hers, and then they found many other places.

Still she was not reluctant in attempting to find out what it was all about. What it was the other girls thought so enjoyable, and the other boys always talked about.

The sudden pain of his thrust was soon gone, and his rhythmic body melted into hers. But the more he became excited, the more she began to hate him. The investigation, the want of knowledge was a sudden surge to pure anger and hatred. She wanted to suddenly push him off, To push him away. To get him off her. To slap him out of her life forever. To slap all men out of her life forever.

She tried.

She tried desperately.

She might have screamed, cursed, shouted. but his lips and tongue kept those terrified, angry sounds to a mini-mum and which were eventually choked back, with her spit, down into her throat. And all of her struggling was held dawn by his strong arms. She was not going to get up from that grassy knoll, a grassy knoll which had suddenly become cold, ugly, until he wanted her to. And he was not going to permit that until he had finished his last thrust, and even then only when he had sufficiently cooled. Then and only then did he rise up and kneel with that dripping thing looking down to her...directly over her lips where a dry tongue attempted to relieve her parched entities. He wanted her to do things with her mouth but she reached up suddenly and tore her nails into that thing and while the creep screamed in tear-filled pain she grabbed up her panties, pulled down her skirt and ran off into the darkness.

No one would ever know who the father of her baby daughter was. Nor would her own father and mother ever know why one bright July day she went off to her graduation class, accept her diploma and disappear. And the girl child would never know either its real mother or its bastard father. And the real mother would never see the child from birth on. That's the way it had to be.

And that's the way Shirley had wanted it!

2

THEIR CAR WAS RED, long, broad, new, and a Cadillac. And it was braked to a slow halt in front of number 9 Devil Lane. In reality the musty old mansion didn't need a number. It was at the end of a cul-de-sac with no other houses...only wild brush, trees, and thickets of an extremely run down area.

Danny turned slowly to Shirley before he turned off the motor. "All we need is night and lightning to set a real horror scene." He glared out the right side of his windshield to the full scene of the house and its ugly surroundings. "Shit, Shirley. You gotta be kidding."

"I've never been more serious in my life." Her eyes held a strange fascination for the old house. "If I'm ever going to solve this problem I certainly need help."

"A psychiatrist has much more pleasant sur-roundings."

"A psychiatrist we've tried. Over and over again we've tried. It hasn't worked."

"So now you want to try the occult."

"Madam Heles is a true spiritualist."

"Madam Heles is a shithead of the first water. Fuck,

Shirley, I can teach you everything you want to know about fuckin'!"

"I wish you wouldn't use words like that!"

"I've been using words like that all my life and I don't plan to change now." He sneered his tones. "Good Christ, broad, you're the reason for us being here...not me!"

She lowered her eyes. "I know...I know." Shirley opened her side of the car and got out. Then stood leaning against the side of the car.

Danny came around the front to join her. He also leaned against the door beside her. "I can think of a hundred better hotels I've stayed at, but for the life of me I can't even dream up one worse."

"It'll only be for a few days, Besides if it doesn't work out we can always leave."

He fluffed up the fur of her pink angora sweater so that the pressure tickled her luscious right tit underneath. She shivered but it wasn't the slightest bit sexually oriented. It was simply the same type of chill she got from a cold wind.

"I'm a cold fish," she had told herself over and over again until she had convinced herself of that selected fact. But the fact remained that whenever a man came within breathing distance of her, the reaction was always the same.

She had tried more desperately with Danny, to love him, to make love to him, to take him to her bed and do all the things a woman should do for her man when in the bedroom action.

Danny was handsome, built like a bull and in the beginning, before they were married it was easy enough to keep him at arm's length distance...except for the necessary kissing which not only cemented their relationship but foretold of interesting things to come in the future...things she knew could never happen...things she so desperately wanted to happen but there was no force within her entire being that could direct itself to that point. She knew sex was a universal happening but it just wasn't happening for her.

Sometimes she wanted to lie back on her pink satin covered bed and cry her eyes out. She'd heard that sexual frustration such as hers had led many young girls and men to suicide. But suicide wasn't even to be her choice. That was as much a crime against God and morality as promiscuous sexual affairs. These were considerations that could never be brought to any serious thought. In her father's house such things were harped upon as much as any other immoral conduct.

"You've got to get over this shaking every time I touch you, Shirley."

She hugged her arms over her breasts. "I know...I know, Danny. But I am trying. That's why we're here, isn't it? To see what can be done?"

"Well," he sighed. "We're getting nowhere standing on the outside looking in."

"You're right about that. Come on!" She led the way across the ancient, scarred, cracked sidewalk, then up a set of rickety worn stairs.

Then they were standing in front of a massive oak door with an age-rusted iron knocker. Danny sighed, shrugged, then lifted the extremely heavy knocker. It banged loudly against a metal receiving plate. The almost terrifying sound echoed, resounded and re-echoed through the hallway beyond the door.

Startled, they looked at each other, but there was no answer to the knock. Danny repeated the deafening procedure several times more with still no answer. Shirley reached over and twisted the circular iron door handle and the door creaked open.

They entered into a musty smelling hall. Dust was thick everywhere...on all the ancient furniture...relics of some bygone age. Cobwebs hung loosely from a high ceiling, and the rug which captured their feet had long since seen its useful days. Bits of the material chipped off with each step they took...and the material changed quickly to more dust and it floated through the thick stale air with all the other foreign matter.

Danny stopped with his hand on the inside knob. He watched as Shirley inched forward. "It's my thought that we shouldn't be doing this. The fuzz might consider it breaking and entering."

"Honestly, Danny," Shirley stormed al him but did not raise her voice. "Sometimes I think you're more of an old woman than my mother." The disgust was all in her tone not the volume.

His eyes glanced over the shadowed hall again, trying to pierce even the darkest corners. "I just don't like to think of going to jail. It's not a very pleasant place to spend a vacation, I understand. Closed doors have always held the feeling of being trapped to me. I mean, except bedroom doors." He took her arms to lightly hold back her forward motion. "People sometimes get mad when you walk all over their houses."

"Oh, come on Danny! We're invited guests!"

"Then where's the inviters?"

"Oh be quiet and close the door."

Danny creaked the door closed behind him, but there was a loud click...a lock...almost the sound of some sort of finality which caused both of them to make a double take. "Any minute I expect Dracula or the Frankenstein monster to come waltzing down their corridors."

They continued down the length of the hall until a particularly daring cobweb drifted down from the ceiling and Danny had to fight his way out of it. "Good shit...let's add the Mummy and the Wolfman to those I expect."

Then they faced a thick purple velvet drape that covered the end of the hall. "It's the only way to go," blinked Danny, as Shirley took a big intake of breath. It was loud...a gasp. She then held her breath until regular breathing was restored.

Danny hadn't turned his head at her sounds. His eyes remained on the thick velvet curtains as if searching for the opening. It was dead center. He put both his hands to the folds and carefully pulled each side apart...just enough so that one eye could peep through. He did a quick double take, snapped the curtains shut, then just as speedily opened them again.

"What is it?"

"What did you say this place was?"

"Madame Heles' establishment..."

"Yeah. Yeah...I know. A necromancer's joint. The home of the witch! Well good shit, this place is an undertaker's joint." He threw open the curtains to reveal the further room.

It was immaculate in reds and backs. And at the far end among fresh flowers and plants was a dark bronze coffin affixed on top of a black velvet covered bin. And in the front of the bin was a black velvet covered ceremonial altar with silver ceremonial goblets and a human skull, the hideous eye sockets staring vacantly...the bone-like teeth in the ancient jaw appeared as if they might still be able to snap at its victims.

Behind the entire arrangement was a silver, inverted cross.

Danny entered the room. Shirley quickly took him by the arm, her protection...of sorts.

"I'm scared," she whispered.

"You're sure as hell the one who wanted to come here...witches be damned."

"I didn't know it would be anything like this." She shuddered. "Caskets...and...and...all this other stuff." Shirley looked directly to him. "Danny...I'm scared...scared almost stiff."

"Shit...girl."

"There you go again." She slammed her arms down from his. "Your mouth should taste like...well, what you keep saying."

"Shit." He put his hands, doubled up fists on the upper portion of his hips. The defiance wasn't directed toward Shirley. It was directed to the shimmering mortician's Cadillac of a departure vehicle. "'Course I never been one to open things like Pandora's Box but," then he did eye her carefully, "if boxes are what we expect to open around here, then boxes will be opened." He reached over and tickled her through the thin mini skirt...at her crotch area.

Shirley ducked back a step...swiftly. "Why did you do that?"

Danny laughed. "Boxes. Don't you get it? Open Pandora's box...? Shirley's box...?"

Shirley's eyes blazed...but she didn't have a chance to answer as the musical voice greeted their ears.

"I am Tanya!"

Their eyes snapped to the new direction...the sound of the voice which was all music...oozed sex...held the expectations of things to come...foretold of future promises.

Tanya was naked except for a sheer red babydoll negligee which was tied at a point just below and directly between each beautifully pink, rosebud tipped breast. Her fiery red pubic proved the red of her head hair was all it professed to be. No dye in the universe could prove two points of value in such an exquisite rendezvous of perfection.

She was not without her touch of the macabre, however. Her babydoll negligee was trimmed in black lace. And her sparkling dark brown eyes glistened in her strange welcome.

Tanya, her hands cupped in the inverted sign of the Devil's prayer, approached the young couple and once more Shirley's arms and hand locked themselves through Danny's again. He felt her shiver and this time he patted her hand.

"She's Tanya," he finally stumbled out the words. "Shsssssssssh," Shirley cautioned, then turned to the fantastically beautiful body in front of them. "We're the Carpenters."

Tanya moved closer to them, her hands still in the pose of inverted prayer. She nodded. "You are expected!" She nodded again. The eyes twinkled again. Danny was sure he saw her pubic hair twitch...but it could have been an optical illusion...a hell of an optical illusion of course...a something that wasn't there...or was it?

Shirley caught the look. "What are you looking at?"

"Tanya's...Pandora's box."

Shirley might have answered. Tanya, however unclasped her hands. "Madame Heles does not receive guests until the hour of midnight is upon uh."

Danny eyed the bronze coffin. "The horror picture bit again." He wasn't laughing.

Tanya wasn't laughing either. "We will attempt to make your stay comfortable...for these two days."

Shirley couldn't think of anything else to say. "We're most anxious to meet Madame Heles."

The twinkle again offered. "Most are!" Then a serious glow seemed to appear throughout her entire nakedness. "But..." She held to a dramatic pause. "But that cannot be until midnight. You will be called!!!"

Danny snapped up his wristwatch. "Good shit!"

Shirley glared.

Danny couldn't give a damn. "It's only two-thirty in the afternoon. What in hell do we do in the meantime?"

Again the gleam. "A room has been assigned you!"

3

THERE WERE an entire maze of halls and rooms, no more confusing and limiting to Shirley and Danny than the outer main hall had been. But the bedroom Tanya led them into was one of the most gracious they had ever seen. It was decorated in variations of gold with the bed spread done completely in gold-dyed fox fur...deep and expensive.

Shirley let her hand run through the soft fibers as she and Danny moved to the opposite side of the King-sized bed. "I've never seen anything like it."

"Inviting, isn't it?"

"You can say that again."

Danny eyed the lovely Shirley. "How would you know?" Tanya looked to him quickly. "She will know. As you shall also know. All things within the walls of this establishment are for the purpose of learning. All of life...all that is important in life is here to be digested and counter studied. There is much about sex which no text book can ever relate. Who of us ever wish to force our eyes to read and our minds to attempt concentration on the musty volumes hidden away so well on dusty library shelves? Volumes written over the ages by the medical men who wrote in words few of them could ever understand.

"These volumes, however, perhaps were not for the layman to read. They were references for yet another medical man or the medical student. The layman need not know anything about his creation other than what he is told...only what they want him to know.

"The layman was to be left in the dark about his sex life. If it were to be known, the churches of old and still many of the present, held alternatives that sex was for one simple reason, propagation of the races...and it was not to be an enjoyable sensation..."

Shirley thought back, and she could again almost hear the same type of words coming from her father's lips. It seemed strange to hear them being issued through the shiny, blood red lips of this beautiful woman of the world.

"Indeed," Tanya continued. "Heads could and did roll for many of those daring enough to have promiscuity in their sex lives. Harlots, women of every vintage and sometimes simple, lovely housewives found themselves chained to a stake and burned alive while their lover was turned into a eunuch before their very eyes.

"The husband was permitted to have intercourse with his wife only for the purpose of having children. If anything felt good about the affair, meaning of course the climax, then they were not to acknowledge it...and Lord forbid that there was ever any love play as a prelude to the affair. Once the wife was impregnated she was not to be touched again until the birth took place. This was the law.

"In some religions the wife was dressed entirely, her entire body in coarse sackcloth. There was only a small hole over her pubic region to where the male would insert his penis. This was to aid in keeping the possibility of enjoying the affair at a minimum.

"Homosexuality between males, lesbianism between females, any of the deviations were outlawed on penalty of death. Intercourse was solely to beget more offspring, especially males...they were all future soldiers, cannon fodder for the overlords who could have sex any way, shape or form they wanted. It was their birthright. The peasants should have nothing to make them comfortable or to give them any pleasure out of life. They were considered as nothing more than a herd of cattle.

"Cattle were mated, then slaughtered and food was obtained. Then should the human herd be any different? A different sort of food for the rulers.

"Knowledge of his own sex life and what makes one enjoy one thing and another something totally different has been a deep dark secret for years. Those in power are always frightened when they feel the herd might learn too much about anything. Since sex is the motivating force in the whole universe then that MUST be the entity which MUST be held in the strictest of secrecy.

"It has been so only until these very recent times. When people started to realize they wanted to know what it was all about. People were getting hung up and couldn't understand why...what caused them...frustration...mental blocks. In some cases pure insanity has developed through sexual inadequacies...the ultimate horror of all sexual encounters...frustration...

"There will be no frustrations when you are ready to leave here." Tanya dropped her hand to the gold fur covering. "I trust you will be comfortable here."

"Even our own bedroom at home isn't as lovely as this." Shirley mirrored Tanya's move in that she let her hand go to the fur coverlet and permitted her fingers to entwine themselves in the luxurious fur.

"Madame Heles feels her guests should be comfortable at all times." She pointed to a set of bright red pajamas on a gold fur-covered chair. "Pajamas for you, if you wish them." Tanya had eyed Danny, then as she turned to Shirley she indicated a sheer, two-toned pink nightie...a floor length affair. "The pink is for you. We must always think of our bodies as exotic. Your exotic body will not be hidden when you wear that one. It will enhance all of your delights...

"Entire nudity is not always a MUST in this house. At times the delicate materials leave something to be wondered about."

"It's lovely. "

"We know many of the things our clients prefer even before they enter through our portals. Madame Heles sees all and we are always prepared."

Danny laughed. It was a nervous laugh, but a laugh all the same. "What makes you think I'll look good in red nylon?"

"Red is for blood. Red is for courage. Many times we find both useful here." She reached to a hidden compartment on the side of the headboard and when her hand came into sight again it was holding what Danny knew to be a giant, life-like soft plastic dildo, complete with testicles. "There will be those to serve you and service you. All you have to do is squeeze this DORK and your call will he answered. "

She squeezed the testicles and although there was no sound she turned to the door through which they had entered.

"You require service?" The voice nearly sang.

"Simply a demonstration this time, Paula." She looked to Danny pointedly"

"These are the Carpenters. They will be spending a few days with us. Paula will be YOUR immediate servant...for anything." Then she snapped her fingers and Paula went out, closing the door behind her.

Danny wiped his forehead. "Do...do they all look like her around here?"

Tanya smiled. "Some are prettier...all are beautiful."

Danny whistled!

Shirley glared!

Tanya grinned! "We will talk again."

"Before midnight?" Shirley was nervous.

"Many things can happen before midnight..." She crossed to the door and took the ornate handle in her delicate fingers, then turned to face the young couple again. "Until midnight, then."

Danny made his usual movement...doubled up fists on his hips. "Where else would we be?"

Tanya used the sensuous gleam again. "That, of course, would be up to you to tell me, wouldn't it, friend Danny Carpenter?"

"Now what in hell do you mean by that?" He crossed closer to her over a quick, silent protest by Shirley and the raising of her arm to his. "Look, pretty broad. The only thing you've said that sounded like sense all the time we've been here is that long spiel about ancient history...and you couldn't prove its authenticity by me. Everything else is parables or a lot of gunk about some mysterious MADAM. Well shit girl, I'm going to want some damned straight answers and I mean fuckin' quick, or I pack my balls and get out of here." He swung his arm and pointed a quick finger at Shirley without looking in her direction. He had captured Tanya's eyes and he wasn't about to easily let them go. "And that goes for her too. I'll pack up her cunt and it goes out of here with me. Maybe she's got a sealed-up cunt, but she can still walk out of here with it between her legs. At least she'll know it's still there even if she don't know how to use it." He switched his hand back to point a finger under Tanya's nose. Silently, but pointedly, she brushed it away. "Straight answers. That's what I'm going to demand from here on in or somebody's fuckin' ass is going to be in a ringer."

"There are many types of ringers, Danny."

"Mr. Carpenter."

Hard! "Danny."

Tanya turned and left the room.

4

DANNY STRETCHED out on the bed and put his hands under his head. His eyes turned to watch Shirley lower her skirt and put it neatly over the gold fur-covered vanity seat. She was talking to him but not looking directly at him. "You shouldn't have talked to her that way."

"Just what in the fuck way should have I talked to the bitch? Do you think I was born just before I came through that door. Baby I know exactly what this place is and you better get it through your head what it is. Call it what you want...necromancer...witch...shit, girl. It's nothing more than an old fashioned whorehouse... just like the ones my father told me about that he went to with his five bucks...sometimes three bucks...during World War II. Since then all they've done is change the approach. I can show you massage parlors with fancy names too, but it all boils down to simple whorehouses. A whorehouse by any other name is a whorehouse. And that...that Tanya or whatever in hell her name is, is nothing more than one of the prostitutes...and that maid...boy, there's a number. So she's the piss maid. You can bet your stinking crap she'll do anything she's asked to do...for a price. God Damn it!!! Everybody around here is available for a price!"

Shirley pulled the pink angora sweater up over her head, then folded it neatly and put it with the skirt.

"You're the most cynical man I've ever met. I don't know sometimes why I'm willing to go through all this for you."

"Sure you do! It's because you love me." He started to take his tie off.

"You're saying that in jest of course, but you know it's true." She watched him toss the tie to a long couch across the room.

"Ah, I don't like this whole lock-up." He came to the edge of the bed to remove his trousers, which he kicked across to join the tie. He wore no undershorts... and his flaccid penis lay out to Shirley's cold stare.

She quickly diverted her eyes and unfastened her brassiere. The garment would join the skirt and sweater on the vanity seat. "I admit it's a strange place. But strange happenings come from strange surroundings."

"Strange! That's the understatement of the century. I'm starting to think this whole fuckin' lash-up is just one big hallucination. I've got to be dreaming, having a helluva horrible nightmare. There's just no place in reality for something like this. Shades of Hades...it's impossible." He took off his shirt and it too sailed across the room to the couch. "If I thought all it would take is a scare to get you around to enjoying a good fuck, I'd have taken you to all the horror movies available. And another thing!" He pointed his finger at her. "What in hell do you think will happen if they find out we've never fully consummated our marriage." He snapped down his hand.

"They won't, if you don't tell them. Besides we won't ever unless I can be cured of all these fixations."

"There's the word...fixations. You've already made a step forward. You know and admit what's wrong with you. Just like alcoholics have to admit they're alcoholics before they even have a chance of being cured."

"Oh Danny, why do you always have to put such things on a clinical basis?"

"Well, don't those shitty medical magazines put all sex down as something clinical?"

She lowered her head. "Not all of them!"

Danny thought he'd won his point. "But most of them, huh!"

"Not...Not the ones those girls showed around the beauty parlor the last few times." She was really blushing a true pink.

Danny got the full impact. He started to laugh. "Turned you on, huh?" He laughed again, and sat stark naked on the edge of the bed. "Real fuck stuff?"

"They...they...in the pictures...were doing that...and other things. I had to close my eyes."

"Shit, girl...that's about the time you should have been keeping them open." Exasperated. "Now, when in the hell are you going to realize that's the type of thing you've got to start with. You don't turn on with a guy right there in front of you...so undoubtedly it's going to take something else...maybe the pictures..." And his voice trailed off as Shirley's mind drifted back...

TO...

———

SHE HAD BEEN VERY YOUNG, fourteen, and there had been a church picnic. There were always church picnics...endless sandwich making and eating... endless root beer and lemonade...endless kids and their silly games...endless screams of terror and pleasure as the kids hit the very cold water of Kripple Bush Creek...

There were always the fathers and the mothers. Fathers guarding their language whenever the preacher was within hearing distance. The mothers, seemingly. always busy at the picnic table and completely, gushingly flustered when the preacher directed any particular word to them...expected smiles and grins that were difficult to form...words which were equally as difficult to form. Who knows what the preacher might think is said or done in bad taste?

"Fuck you!" muttered a red-nosed man who had brought along his secret jug. "Fuck you!" and his wife shit her cotton drawers, then went off to say silent prayers of forgiveness.

Shirley had worn a light yellow cardigan over her plain white blouse and yellow skirt. The hot July day certainly didn't call for a sweater of any kind, but she'd always had a strange fetish for any knitted garments. No matter what degree the weather, she could be counted on to have a sweater with her even if she was only carrying it. Fact was it became sort of a trademark for her. In the beginning when this fact was realized by the other kids they teased her a lot, but when they saw she wore them like a badge of honor, the chiding stopped and her proudness grew. Moreso to the boys who voyeuristically couldn't take their eyes from the sweater front. Shirley had developed by the middle of her thirteenth year.

"Whow, you look good in sweaters," was one of the more mild approaches which had been directed at her throughout her high school years.

But she hated those forced picnics. There had to be something else which could be done on a Saturday afternoon. The world couldn't be made up of one big Saturday picnic. She walked, alone, through the woods and wondered what other people, beyond the tight limits of Kripple Bush did with their Saturday afternoons.

She knew the little kids enjoyed themselves and many of the teenage boys and girls looked like they were enjoying themselves...they were generally holding hands and always there was, what she thought, a look of some kind of anticipation in their eyes...and many of them were seen to drift away from the main group for long walks in the woods...and they were always giggling when they returned...giggling from some kind of private secret.

Shirley also took her long walks in the woods. Who was afraid of snakes...? So the Catskill Mountains of upstate New York were infested with copperheads and rattlers. She'd never seen one. Any old snake who bothered her would find itself with its head cut off.

The breeze, hot but cooling at the same time, drifted through her soft hair and the hair delightfully tickled her ears. She didn't mind the picnics at such times. She was alone and seemingly at peace with the world.

There was only the sounds of the virgin woods. Nature sounds all around her. And something else that particular time.

A soft rustling from behind some thick brush... brush where on the other side she knew there was an indentation in the earth...a soft, grassy, bed-like affair where she herself had lain many times as she looked up at the blue sky and soft white cotton clouds.

But it was her spot and something was there disturbing the tranquility. She parted a section of the brush softly, silently, so as not to disturb whatever was there. There would be no disturbing the creature who lay there...the two human creatures she knew as Billy Haney and Sheila Apperson.

Billy had on only his swim trunks and Shirley could see his stiff snake crawling out through the leg opening. Sheila's short summer dress was pulled way up around her neck so that her youthful, pink budded breasts stared toward the sky. Her panties were intact, pink nylon, and snug fitting around her hips and luscious fanny. But the damp spot at the crotch was all too noticeable.

The young couple were suddenly locked in each other's arms, their lips smashing together in loud sucking sounds...their bodies crushing together and gyrating to each other. There were soft moans and whispered words which were meant only for them to hear. And Billy's hands fastened first on the right breast then the left, and always there was a kneading motion to his hands.

Sheila's hands weren't empty either. She had let her left hand drift down to his rigid cock. "Kiss it...kiss it, Sheila. Put your mouth on it...suck it dry.'"

The girl blinked. "I've never done it that way before."

"It won't bite. Suck me off. All the girls are doing it that way. Mary will only suck guys off. She won't fuck nobody with her cunt because she's scared of getting knocked up. You're better than her in every way. You're prettier. You got a prettier cunt, prettier ass, and by far the prettiest tits in the whole school. God damn, what pretty fuckin' tits you do have. Sometime I'm going to put my prick between them and fuck hell out of them. Bet you ain't never had anything like that neither."

All the time Sheila masturbated him. "You won't cum in my mouth," she panted.

"Naw," he assured her. "Not a chance. I like the cum in your cunt best of all."

"If you knock me up you'll have to marry me."

"You ain't never got knocked up any of the other times. Why should my cum to your cunt knock you up this time?" Sheila turned around so that her crotch lay near his face and her lips were but an inch from the head of his penis, her hand still in motion on the shaft, "I do like that big cock of yours."

"Sure you do, honey."

"Will it ever get any bigger?"

"You can bet on it."

She touched the purple, blood throbbing head of his dork with her tongue. The cock jumped once, like it was suddenly startled out of a sound sleep. Then she looked to him.

"Will you lick my cunt if I suck your prick?"

He didn't answer her with words. He simply buried his face deep into her pubic region and his tongue made sloshing sounds. Sheila's eyes closed in ecstasy from the first lick and her body began to shiver and her thighs twitched with the further tongue swipes.

If she had been reluctant before there was no longer any possibility she would turn away. She drove the head full into her mouth and she gave a sudden moan of pure delight...as if she had found a joy never before experienced. Then it appeared she really hungered for the meat. Sheila went at it with every muscle her lips, mouth and tongue could muster.

Billy turned slowly over on his back, She followed

his move with her own body. She buried his face into her furry crotch and she never missed a stroke on his swelling, throbbing cock.

Shirley wanted to tear herself away from her place of concealment...but the demand to watch was much more powerful. The fascination of what she saw made her own crotch twitch, grow warm then sweat until little rivulets seeped through the legs of her own panties. She felt a tremendous urge to urinate even though she knew she'd squatted and done just that only a few minutes before along the trail.

Sheila was working more furiously than ever. Her head bobbed up and down the shaft and over the head faster and faster, and her hand squeezed the balls like squeezing a soft sponge. Then she was gagging and choking, but still never missed a stroke as the boy whispered huskily, "Good God, I'm coming...suck it...bite it...suck it. Take it all. Eat my cum. Swallow it. Don't pull out now. Eat it. You'll kill me if you stop now. Swallow it." His head thrashed from side to side as his screamed whisper echoed into her cunt.

Sheila couldn't have stopped at that moment even if she wanted to. Billy's lashing tongue, then words of excitement stirred her own exciting climax. Climax after climax. Her climaxes came one beat before his. She wanted to yell out her own joys...her own feelings, but she couldn't. Her mouth was too full of cock...then a spurting cock as the cum sprayed the entire interior of her mouth, then slid down her hot throat. She didn't gag as she worried she might have. But there was so much of the juice that some seeped between her lips and drained along the shaft.

Sheila sucked it dry before she finally rolled away. Then her hand reached down and she inserted her middle finger into her own cunt. The loose ends of her torn panty crotch caressed the back of her hand as she fingered herself.

Billy could only lay back with his flaccid penis and watch her through blurred, glazed eyes. But his hand went to the limp dick and stroked it hopefully. It was all too apparent he really did want to shove his shaft into her hole.

"I'll be ready soon," he feigned.

"I know," Sheila breathed softly, and her head moved slowly, ecstatically from side to side as she first fingered her clitoris, then jammed in and out of her vagina.

Finally her luscious fanny slammed several times into the soft grass and her further moans told of the powerful climaxes she was experiencing. Then she lay in his arms again, his limp dick crushed to her pubic region through the torn panties.

"Kissing and sucking is one thing, but there's nothing like a good fuck. And I don't mean a finger fuck!" She forced her lips fiercely across his and for the first time in Billy's young life, he found out what his own cum tasted like.

5

THEY LAY SIDE BY SIDE, but not close, for a long time. Shirley had slipped into the sexy, sheer pink nylon nightie, but Danny had not bothered to put on the red nylon pajamas. First of all, he didn't like red, and secondly, he didn't ever wear anything to bed.

"You're about as useless as tits on a boar." He rolled over, turning his back to her.

Shirley frowned. "You don't do so bad yourself."

"I never had any complaints before I married you." He snap rolled back to face her. "You know...maybe some of those magazines are really telling it like it is. Maybe all studs and broads should give it a file of whacks before they tie the knot through any preacher."

"People aughtta' fuck and suck a hell of a long time before the'y do anything as serious as marriage. Man, that's the last filled straw and who can suck through a stopped-up straw?"

"Please don't torture me any more, Danny."

"Torture? Me torture you? Good God, Shirley! What in hell do you think you're doing to me?" He grabbed his limp dick in his hand and flopped it back

31

and forth several times. "Look at this limp noodle." Then he grabbed his hard, aching balls. "You know what I got here in my hand? Well I'll tell you. Aching nuts, that's what. Aching nuts...hard rocks we used to call them in the Nave. Nuts all worked up and full of cum that can't be spilled through a limp dick.

"I look at you and see one of the most beautiful broads in the world. Pale pink skin...lips as red as fire... eyes so blue they could make the Pacific Ocean jealous. You've got the tits photographers dream of. You've got a split beaver that makes my tongue sweat...and what do you do with all those luxuries? You hide them behind a facade of shit nobody can understand.

"Torture, Shirley! These hard rocks of mine are turning blue from filling and not being able to have a release. A man's got a lot of cum stored inside of him and it's got to come out. And I stopped beating my meat a hundred years ago. Pretty girl, I've got to get my rocks off and I mean get them off in you...in your cunt."

Shirley buried the side of her face in the crook of her arm. She had turned her back to him in a silent withdrawal.

"Good Lord, Shirley, men and women have been doing it...SEX...since the beginning of time and enjoying it. That's all part of life."

Shirley turned quickly to him. "Then why do people always treat the subject as dirty?"

"What one person thinks is dirty might have a different effect on somebody else. Like sucking a cock..." Shirley shuddered, but Danny continued. "Now sucking a cock is supposed to be dirty...talking about it even dirtier. I bet you've never sucked a cock in your life. 'Course you haven't. Why? Because you've always heard that doing such a thing was dirty, abnormal, perverted.

Well, if it's so God damned dirty, abnormal, perverted, then why is most of the entire world skilled at it? What in hell do you think most broads do for their guys when they're having their monthlies?"

Shirley lay back on the soft pillow and put her hands under her head. Her eyes gazed up at the ceiling. She wished she could at least become angry, but even that emotion eluded her. She felt lonely in a world of people...completely empty inside. She wanted that release as much as Danny, but that something so deep in her mind always singled a red light. If only the yellow would flash so that she could know it would soon turn to green.

She knew Danny was still talking, but his voice had become a dull hum from somewhere in the far away distance...perhaps even the far away past. She honestly didn't approve of those feelings but they had been with her all the days and nights of her life. The Lord knew she had tried everything she could think of. She knew sex was an important fact of everyday make up...and most of the people she had met since leaving home demanded it of themselves.

She hated the 'cold fish' label which had been stuck on her ever since school days. She knew a lot of the other girls were making out with the boys. And it wasn't always in the woods at the church picnics either. She also couldn't figure out the strange curiosity which caused her voyeuristic tendencies. She could have walked away anytime she wanted. She didn't have to wait around and see the entire session, but she did.

Shirley had hiding places under the grandstand at the ballpark. The darkness beyond the diamond was a favorite place for the young lovers. Then there was a 'Lover's Lane,' out by 'Lover's Leap.' The cliff got its name because a couple of Indians, a young boy and girl, ended their illicit love affair there. Some might have believed it was kind of a morbid place to have sex. But then, most of the young people had a morbid sense of humor and it bled over into their sneaked sexual affairs.

It was 'Lover's Lane' where she saw her first lesbian affair. However it took her a long time to realize what it was they were doing to each other...or what kind of kicks two girls could get out of each other. In later years she learned the terms 'Butch' and 'Fluff,' but right then it was simply two young, very pretty girls. There was Mona who was rather tall but had very little front to fill out her sweater. But she was otherwise a doll to look at. And there was Sally who had beautiful long blonde hair which stretched far down her back. She always wore soft, frilly dresses during the summer.

And there they were sitting in the back seat of Mona's car. It was her own car. In fact she was the only one in the school who owned her own car clean and clear. It had been a birthday gift from her father who was a high-priced lawyer.

Shirley watched them carefully from her place of concealment. First they were simply kissing. But not a kiss of pure friendship as girls will do. They seemed to be setting each other on fire with their slashing tongues...and their hands were all over the front of each other. Mona's hands were especially active and pointed in their moves. Her right hand went deep into the low cut neckline of Sally's dress and Shirley knew Mona was doing the same thing to Sally's breasts as a boy would do.

Then they were panting and talking softly but heatedly...and their searing body fires caused them to quiver and shake...a hand went here...the lips met...then more feeling.

"Suck my titties, please suck my titties, Mona." Sally was almost cooing.

Mona reached into the low neck line and brought the youthful, firm breasts into full view with the dress neckline being underneath. Her tongue tickled the nipple for a long while, then she licked the entire globes for an even longer time before she finally sucked the entire orb into her mouth. Sally gave a squeal of delight and snapped her right hand down her front. A finger slipped into the leg opening of her panties. She began fingering herself frantically.

"Don't take it away from me," breathed Mona over the breast. "Whatever you do, don't take it away from me." She hungered for the juicy cunt but she was also reluctant to give up the breast sucking as yet. Mona liked a lot of foreplay with the girl's body before she would bring her tongue to play on the clitoris. There had been other girls, many girls, in Mona's young life, but she liked Sally best of all. She certainly had the most luscious body of all.

"I won't...I won't take it from you. It's yours...all yours. I'm all yours. My body...my insides...my burning cunt is always all yours." Her finger was working furiously. Her head twisted from side to side. Her eyes were closed in the ecstasy of the moment, and the feeling. Her own free hand came up to mash and knead the breast which Mona wasn't working on. She hadn't taken that one out of the dress. She liked the feel of it through the material, Sally had never been one for getting completely nude during any of her sex acts. If it were known Sally had a tremendous clothes fetish. She had to have at least some of her clothing on in order to climax. She would feel them, love them, and strange illusions would race through her mind, then transfer into electrical shocks which traveled the length of her nervous system then buried itself deep within her vagina canal and waited to be discharged.

And if it were also known the whole clothing fetish stemmed from the fact that whenever she had sex there was the chance of discovery. Therefore keeping her clothes on lessened the possibilities of what the real session was all about. She could simply drop her dress or pull in her chest and her titties would snap back into place under the dress.

Even when she wore cardigan sweaters, buttoned up the front she never unbuttoned them. She'd simply pull them up around her neck for the titties exposure.

Then she suddenly found herself about to climax. She took her finger out of the wet, sticky vagina and spread her legs wide apart.

"Grab it, for God sake Mona get down there and lick it. Lick the piss out of it."

Mona lowered her whole body instantly. She made quick work of slipping Sally's panties. Then she lowered her face deep into the soft fur of Sally's pubic region. Her tongue smashed in and out of the juicy box. With each stroke Mona made sure she also attacked the clitoris, both on the inward and the outward movement. And on each contact with the ,'little man in the boat' Sally shuddered with anticipation and delight. Actually she was shaking all over with the sex thrills. She liked sex. She'd rather be in a sex situation than do anything else in the entire world.

She had tried it a few times with boys around the school, but boys were a frightening entity to her. Their big pricks had hurt her from the very first insertion when her cherry was taken.

Then too there was always the horrible thoughts of getting knocked up. She'd often thought if such a thing ever happened to her she'd go over 'Lover's Leap.' But that was not to happen. She found lesbian love with Mona.

Then she gave an extra loud, prolonging moan and gurgle. Her legs tightened around Mona's head and held her in place. Her ass bounced up and down on the car seat and Mona dug her face, her chin, her lips, her tongue, her nose deep into the cleft. Mona licked furiously. She smashed the tongue back and forth, over and over again in ever increasing speeds. Sally's entire body swung from side to side as orgasm after orgasm wracked her body. She seemed to have a never-ending flow of jerking delights...then they slowly subsided and Mona pulled her face back from the fur-like fur. She traveled up the length of Sally's body and poised her lips scarce inches from her mouth.

"Kiss me, my darling Sally. Kiss me and taste your own sweet cunt!"

Sally reached out quickly and took the back of Mona's head with both her hands. They drove their lips tightly together...their mouths open to accept each other's tongues. It was a long sound-accompanied piece of action. Their spits and Sally's cunt juice mixed in gulping delights.

Then it was Sally's turn. She pulled her lips from Mona's and there was a sparkle in her eyes. "Sometime maybe we can have a bed."

"It might look strange for us to get a motel room. We're too young. Somebody would surely check."

"I know...I know...I only wish my folks would go

away on their vacation and leave me behind. God, wouldn't that be fun. We could suck and dildo fuck for two whole weeks and have that entire big house to do it in. God, how I love your tongue up inside of me like that. Sometimes I think I'm going to blow my whole mind and it will come right out of that little hole down there. Right out and all over your tongue so that you could swallow it and I'd be more than ever inside of you. That's what I really wish. I wish I could be so deep inside of you." Then Sally kissed Mona another prolonged, open-mouthed sticky kiss.

"Get inside of me now," moaned Mona, then stretched out on her back and pulled up her skirt and took off her own panties.

But Sally didn't go immediately to work with her tongue in that lower position. She pulled up Mona's sweater and took the breasts. Mona wore no brassiere and although her breasts were very small, they were well formed and exactingly pointed with large nipples. Sally kissed them lovingly, then she sucked at them and rubbed them all over her own face. She took the nipple up to her eyes and used her eyelids as if she were winking the nipple off. Then she tickled the inside of her ear with the nipples.

Mona's naked belly button was just above the skirt line and it was the next base of attack for Sally, who was slowly working her way down the length of Mona's body. She had made a light river of spit, with her tongue, down the naked portion of the lovely girl's body, and it finally ended in the soft cunt hairs where Sally's long hair hid her face from sight.

But the sounds Mona made, and the slurping and sucking sounds that came from the scene told Shirley that the same thing was happening to Mona as had happened to Sally. Then there was the searing climax. But Mona didn't appear to have as many climaxes as Sally had had. But they also seemed to be more powerful. Mona's legs shot out like shapely spears with each orgasm.

Then the load was spent and they lay back in each other's arms again. "Now you can taste your own cunt, lover." Sally buried her lips and open mouth in Mona's.

6

DANNY DID his damndest and Shirley attempted her pathetic best but all that was aroused was Danny's renewed ire. During that past hour ire had worked himself to a weak, sweating unsatisfied babbling idiot who had to turn away and lay less than spent, back on the wet, crumpled sheets. He stared at the gold ceiling for a long time as did Shirley.

Then Danny growled at the wall but directed his words at Shirley. "I might just as well have been watching television...that's about how much of a charge you give me."

"Maybe you have something to do with it. Maybe you just don't try hard enough."

"Hard, that's the whole problem damn it, You can't get me hard enough and you can't even take a soft on."

Tanya had listened through the hidden peep hole in the eye of an owl...a painting which hung over the bed. She was smiling broadly, knowingly as she made her way back through the maze of corridors until she was once more in the coffin room.

She crossed the spacious, thick rug and folding her

hands in an inverted prayer style, she knelt down in front of the altar and poured herself a large dose of the ceremonial wine which she downed slowly, but kept her eyes on the bronze casket all the time she drank. And when she replaced the cup to the altar she mumbled several words in a weird prayer. These she did with her eyes rightly closed.

Then she did a strange thing. She picked up the skull head with one hand and with the other untied the bow of her red, black lace trimmed shortie negligee and it fell open on both sides. Her fantastically luscious breasts came into full view and she cupped the left one with her left hand and lowered the skull mouth to the nipple of the right.

"Suck it, oh lost one of this world. Suck it as you would have when you had soft lips and searing tongue. Suck it until I cum without the pressure of a penis within my vagina. Suck it until the sweat from my steaming nipples spills down your skinless chin. Then she changed hands and held the right breast with her right hand and the skeleton resting in her left hand was attached to the left nipple. She repeated the same words then added, "Take them both...take them both oh lost spirit...lost to the endless reaches of the dark, ebony emptiness of eternity. Take them both as if you were still with us in the flesh...then realize you are still with us in spirit and the spirit heat can be more heated than any human because the fires of hell have perhaps already visited upon the skin which once was sewn over the skeleton, and the heat which has torn the spirit from the human."

She lowered the skull to her navel. "Take it and I imagine the tongue which was once there attacking my navel, the most ignored spot on the human body...the spot where so many nerve endings have had their electrical points awaiting so very long for those electricians who know how to connect their own electrons. Wet it with the heat and the water of my own sweat and the nerve ending shocks will be intensified to shocking proportions." She once more lowered it even further until the chin, then the teeth and last, the hollow spot where the nose had been was deeply nestled in her soft fur-like pubic hairs.

"And the shocking proportions will invest themselves to me and to whom ever I direct those sparks. Time for the human is very short upon this planet we call earth and sex is an all consuming universal expectancy. All must feel the fires of hell before they will know they have missed a life which could have been used for more sexual apprehensions...or have they found out by the time the grave is open that they know what it is all about."

Tanya jerked four times in her sudden orgasm and the spasms between each lasted several seconds in between. And during each spasm her eyes closed for the duration then opened again until the next one shook her.

Finally she lowered the skull back to the altar and took up another glass of the wine. She turned slowly to face the bronze coffin and muttered the prayers again. Her hands reached up to retie the black ribbon which clasped her negligee and invertedly formed the prayer sign with her hands, the fingers pointing downward. Her eyes glared at the coffin. "They are as you suspected Madam Heles...unconsummated."

A moan drifted up from the coffin, then a scream which was more of delight than of pain or terror.

At which point Shirley pulled the pink nightie

down over her head and looked down at her husband who was laying on his back, his hands behind his head and his eyes staring at the ceiling. "I'm going to have a look around."

Danny glanced at her. "Do you think your Madam Heles and her cohorts would like you wandering around their whore house?"

"I hate to put anything in your vernacular...but money talks, and yours will talk a long way around here."

"Witches...necromancers...dope that's what they dispense. At the expense of my repeating myself, what in hell makes you think such shit-heads can do anything for either of us, that is if I am wrong about anything myself, which Idoubt?"

"I'm going to look around."

"You said that before."

"Then I guess I'll just go."

"Why in the hell don't you. Let me get some rest. You try my patience. You lead me on, you try to fuck me and you get going and what happens...nothing... always nothing." He sat up on the bed. "Shirley, before I take my cock in my right hand and do what I had to do behind the barn..." and although he continued on, his mind drifted back to that time in his youth...

———

"IT AIN'T the same like you was in the bathtub Jimmy. All us kids get a hard on when we're in the bathtub... maybe it's the hot water, it gets us all worked up." The boy who spoke was Bobby Hepper and he was two years older than Jimmy.

"But you mean you just take it in your hand and it feels just like that...just as good?"

They were walking home from school along the dusty country road and their books were slung across their shoulders held by a tied rope.

"You bet it does, Jimmy. Maybe even better, You mean to tell me you never give that old prick a coupla' licks even when you're in the bathtub...just to get it really going and make sure the juice comes out real good and hard?"

"I...I guess I did."

"Sure you did. And that's the way you do it when you do it when the water ain't there. Only you don't have the water, the hot water down there to get you going in the first place. So you think about something, like the hot water, like when it gets you all worked up. And you stand behind your barn and you take it in your hand and you just...you just jerk off. Like you take it in your hand and you start slow and when you feel it swell you make your hand tighter and pretty soon it gets real hard and you start to feeling real good down there...like there's nothing else and nobody else and there just ain't anything that can make you feel so good down there. Then when you get to feeling like you can't go no further otherwise everything is going to hurt you...that juice just spurts out and goes all over the wall." He paused in his words and took Jimmy's arm and they both stopped momentarily. "Only don't spill none of that juice on your pants or your underwear. It don't come off so good. And you, like when your mother starches your shirt collars for the Sunday shirt...well that's the way that stuff goes to the clothes when it dries...you just can never get it out."

"I'll be careful...but what if somebody catches us

doing something like that. Won't they get awful mad? Maybe they'll even spank us?"

"Shit Jimmy!" And that's where Jimmy grabbed into the expression "Shit." But Bobby Hepper had much more to say. "You don't never take your pants down. You got you fly open."

"Fly?" Jimmy had never heard the expression.

"Fly! Fly!" He pointed to the spot. "The front of your pants where you take your prick out in the school toilet to take a piss. And that's the whole point. You got your fly open and you gotta take a piss. Your dick is hanging out of the front of your fly and you got it in your hand and you're beating the hell out of it. Then supposin' somebody really comes up. All you say is you're taking a piss. Now who is going to stop somebody from taking a pass on the old dirt...? Nobody, that's who. And nobody is going to think anything else about somebody taking a piss. And then you gotta think maybe you want to take your pants down and do it. Put your prick in your hand and you got your pants off. All you gotta do is squat down and it looks like you are taking a shit. Now nobody is going to stop you from taking a shit neither."

Bobby went solemn for a moment as he let go of Jimmy's arm and they started walking again. Then as they walked Bobby looked straight ahead as his words once more spilled from his thick lips.

"I just can't figure why taking out your cock and taking a piss is alright, and you can squat and take a shit just about anyplace you want to is alright, but when you take that prick out of your pants and you can do something with it that makes you feel good...that's all wrong." Again he stopped. "I wonder why if something feels good it's all wrong...but when a piece of shit is too hard and it hurts your ass when it comes out, that's alright?"

"I don't know."

Bobby patted him on the shoulder. "I know you don't...you're too young." His two year advance gave him the superiority of judgement. "But you'll grow up. I guess we all grow up. But there is still a lot of things I guess even older guys like me have to learn." Bobby shook his head. "Maybe even I can find out things before I get as old as my dad."

"Do you think they ever did anything like...?" Jimmy lowered his eyes.

"Go ahead old fellow," braved Bobby. "We guys have to stick together...even if I am a coupla' years older than you are."

"Well I meant, do you think our dads ever went behind the barn like this?" They had reached the back of Jimmy's dad's barn.

"You can bet your marble bag they did. I heard a lot of the guys telling stories about watching things that their fathers and mothers did when they got alone in their bedroom. And their father wasn't doing things alone with their pricks. Their mothers had a lot to do with their hands. And that ain't all. Their fathers take their prick in their hand and put it between their mother's legs."

Jimmy was all wide-eyed. "What happens when they put it between their mother's legs?"

Bobby shrugged. "I don't know. I guess she puts her hands on it and gives their fathers some kind of a good feeling. I guess it must be like something when we do it behind the barn. I guess they must get some kind of a good feeling or otherwise their fathers wouldn't let their mothers do something like taking it in their hands. They gotta be jerking him off somehow."

"Yeah, l guess that's about right. Nobody would let nobody touch that prick if it didn't feel good. Once I caught my prick down underneath me when I sat down to take a shit and it hurt like hell. Only thing that ever hurt me worse was when I caught my balls in the first zipper pants I ever wore. I was sore for a whole week. I turned blue for nearly that whole week. And damn if it would stop bleeding for more than an hour.

"Yeah I hurt myself that way a couple of times. Once I even hurt it when I was jerkinq off. I got so fixed up my hand went back so hard it slammed my balls right into the sides of my legs and I ached all over for a hell of a long time." Bobby looked all around him from their position behind the barn, then he unzipped his pants and took out his penis. He started to stroke it gently. "But there ain't nothing like this." His eyes closed then opened.

Jimmy unbuttoned his Levis and pulled out his own penis and watching Bobby, mirrored his movements.

———

JIMMY IN MADAM HELES' place watched Shirley leave the room, then he shoved off the gold fur coverlet and put his hand around the shaft of his flaccid penis and started the same soft, slow stroke which he had used so many years ago.

7

TANYA MADE HER ROUNDS QUICKLY. She wanted to get it over with. The old ones around the establishment had to be serviced also. But when there were new ones in the house she was always anxious to get started...or at least to observe their movements through the peephole. She had watched Danny and Shirley as long as necessary that first time in order to affix some measure of educational processes that should be directed to them.

But for the moment she was about to be halted in her forward progression. A door near the end of one of the long halls opened and a naked man, not very tall but extremely muscular, stepped out to confront her. He folded his bare arms over his mammoth chest and gazed directly into her eyes which dropped to the hard shaft between his legs.

"That's the damndest tool this establishment has ever seen, Karl." She looked back to him as his hand dropped to surround the shaft.

"And it needs a good sucking and fucking right now, Tanya. You've neglected me all morning."

"You could always have rung for someone else."

"I don't get a good kick with anybody else. You're the one that turned me on and you're the only one who can really make me come off with a bang. All the others do is make me come and I'm all hard and ready to go again. You're the only one that can make me come off where I'm satisfied enough...long enough so that I have time to sit down and eat my dinner or have a cigarette or a cup of coffee. All the others I can take on every minute of the day."

Tanya grinned. "Karl, I do believe you have become insatiable."

"Become, hell, be damned. You made me insatiable. You made me what I am today."

"Whatever you do, don't break into a song."

"I don't sing when I'm not happy."

"And you're not happy?"

He was still holding his cock with his right hand. He then let his left hand shoot downward to grab hold of his balls. He gripped them hard. "How can anybody be happy when they got a set of nuts full of come and a shaft ready to shoot it out. Good God, Tanya! They hurt already."

"I'll call Pauline."

"I don't want Pauline, damn it. I don't want Ruth or Maxine or Tilly or any of the others." He reached over and took her left tit in one hand and encircled her waist with the other and dragged her into him. He crushed her body hard to his. His lips forced themselves upon hers and his crushing tongue pulled her lips apart. Their hot tongues met and Tanya felt the electrical shocks caress the inside of her body. She knew then that she was not going to let the guy go off unsatisfied.

Her own body heats caused the lower portion of her

body to slowly gyrate and she felt the soft ooze of hot sweat leave her pubic hairs and drain down the insides of her legs. Tanya was a hot little piece and the best in the business. But she had always heard that a good whore never got involved with sex or the clients emotionally. But Tanya could never make an affair a cold piece type of thing. When a guy or a girl turned her on, and most of them did, she really enjoyed the affair. She'd rather fuck than eat dinner at any time. She'd rather eat cock than drink any other kind of milk shake. The milk of human gyrations was all she ever looked for, ever wanted.

Karl had been a weak-kneed, milquetoast kind of guy when he had first arrived at the establishment. But when the visit with Madam Heles at her usual midnight arising was over, Karl was turned over fully to Tanya. And Tanya had ways of making the toast burn with delight and the knees strong, so that they could crush a body between them during the blast off of an erotic climax. Karl had never needed the personal services of Madam Heles once he got started with Tanya'

Actually Karl had been one of the more easily converted to a powerful sex life. He got so turned on, he stayed longer than the time he had planned. He was going into his second month residency and was paying rather handsomely for that privilege.

Tanya pulled her lips back, but she let her arms remain around his body and his around hers, crushing her to him. "God, you're a hot tamale," she breathed into his mouth that had remained close to hers.

"You made me this way."

"I suppose I have."

"And you've been neglecting me." He put his hard dick directly through the opening of her negligee material and the throbbing purple head buried itself in the soft cunt hairs which were hot and moist. Tanya's legs jerked at the first touch of the cock, then spasmodically twitched all the time he held it in that position.

"I haven't been neglecting you purposely." She kissed him a peck on his lips, then spoke again. "We have some new and very wealthy clients and they must be serviced also. There are so many others who really could take care of you if you'd only give them a chance. Remember you won't always be here and I won't be with you when you once more go to the outside. You should learn to be satisfied with some of the others. Think of all the girls...and the men on the outside who are waiting for a stud like you. Think of how you'd be cheating them if you couldn't take them on."

"I don't give a shit about anybody but you. Maybe I'll stay here the rest of my life."

"You'd never want to do that because eventually you'd end up in the pit like so many others who couldn't be turned off. Remember if you can't find a turning off point you are lost and gone forever and you could never leave this place."

"I don't want to leave it if I have to leave you. Now come on. I want servicing, and I've got to have it right now." He took his cock in his hand again, and tried to shove the head up into her hole, but she squeezed her vagina lips hard together and he couldn't make an insertion. "Damn it, Tanya, I don't care about any new rich boarders. I got money. I got plenty of money and it's all yours or Madam Heles' as long as I get to fuck who I want. And you're the only one I want to fuck and suck. You taught me about taking on the men. That, of course, was all part of the training period. But give them all back to the Indians.

I want you and I want my cock in your cunt right now."

Tanya sighed. "Very well. At least you're a quickie artist. You won't take me from my rounds for very long. And you really have become an artist. I suppose I can spare the time. But Madam Heles will have to talk to you about further servicing. I can't be on hand for your demands whenever you want me. That has to be understood."

"That all comes later. Now is the present and I need you now!"

Once again he grabbed his shaft and tried to sink his arrow into the moist target. "Not out here in the hall, We'll go into your room."

He dropped his dick, grabbed the girl by the arm and led her quickly back into his room where he raced her across the room and flopped her on the bed bodily.

"Karl, haven't I taught you haste makes waste?"

"Baby, I never waste anything."

Then he dove on top of her and she immediately opened her legs wide to accept the gigantic head of the great, hard tool. And as he drove it home, her eyes seemed to race back into her head. She knew what that thing felt like. She loved it from the first time she had tried it when he came there...when it was still a weak large worm. And she knew it from the first time it really got hard and he learned how to sink it in again and again. And she knew exactly what he would do when the sticky fluid would come gushing through the head and into her.

He would let the last of the pleasures seep through his body, then he would swiftly pull out and he would fall down with his face into that spot between her legs and his long tongue would lick out his own juices that had so quickly mixed with her own. Karl was fast to cum, but Tanya was always ready for the quickie artists. She could hold back or she could let it go. With Karl she let go as quickly as he, and she still had three or four more orgasms than he did. Karl would get plenty of the mixed juices and he would gobble them up with the delights of a kid sucking on an ice cream cone.

Tanya knew that would happen and she stocked his wet back of the neck. There was no doubt that she was getting as much of the joys as he did. She wanted all the feeling she could get also. And when she was under or on top of a guy like Karl, she was in the heights of her erotic, exotic pleasures. And when he had cleaned her out with his fantastic tongue she actually looked forward to cleaning off his wang with her own mouth and tongue. The shaft had been in her and she had tasted the inside of her own pussy many times since she had first laid with a man...and that was when she was thirteen years old...the guy had been a vagabond gypsy who traveled the back roads of the countryside looking for handouts...

Gypsy Louie never worked. He didn't have to. He was a handsome, olive skinned man with a beautifully trimmed mustache. And he was always gaily dressed, something like some of the men of the present. And when his body, clothed in an array of colors and materials, confronted the women who usually saw their men in coarse working clothes or the conventional grey flannels or blue serge, they had to take in sharp breaths... and they had to cross their legs due to the sudden heat which captured their frame...heat, perhaps even more heat, that they had not generated since the first time they had lain with their husbands or lovers.

Gypsy Louie only had to wink his eye and the

women flocked all over him. He always made sure that his approach was made to the homes where he knew the husband was away at work, and most of the suburban women he greeted were sex-starved in the first place. But when the time came that he visited the home of Tanya's mother, the older woman (although quite young) was not home either. The back door was opened by Tanya herself (whose name at that time was Ruth).

The olive-skinned wonder took one look at the beautifully developed girl, and the front of his purple velvet pants stuck out more than six inches. Tanya didn't know at that moment what had happened. But she knew what she felt when he took her in his arms and kissed her a full French kiss on her open mouth. And she knew that her body heats were rising and what that meant because she had felt some of the same type of body heat when she had masturbated, a something she'd been doing almost since she could remember.

Even at that early age Tanya was well developed. She had started to form very early and the budding of her breasts were a delight to her own eyes. No one, not even her own parents, had seen them right up until that time. But the day was hot and she had no brassiere on under the thin summer blouse. Gypsy Louie couldn't take his eyes from the sight and he could almost visualize those orbs and what they would look like even before the blouse came off later. But they were the first thing his hands went to. And because of the delightful feeling she didn't take his hands away.

Tanya had played with her own breasts while she watched the action in her bedroom mirror. This had been something she did almost nightly, and every time, for a long time, before she masturbated. She liked the way her hands felt over the mounds. She helped them along when they were just beginning to grow. In fact, she believed their firmness came from the proper care, the gentle rubbing and massaging she had given them during that period. And she would also always squeeze the nipples between her first two fingers, which she believed gave her the half inch point of a nipple. She loved to watch the nipple grow hard and later, after Louie, and during Louie, when she went to school she liked to rub up the nipple under her blouses and especially under her sweaters so that the point made a great mark on the sweater front. She loved to turn on the boys, and if she turned on a few of the girls...what was the harm? Girls liked to be turned on by other girls some of the time. There was a definite envy in their eyes at such times...even the latent lesbians who didn't know they were going to be lesbians by the time they got out of school.

But Gypsy Louie was to be the first man to ever take her into the realm of sexual intercourse. And it was that first day when he came to the door and her mother wasn't home.

"You're such a pretty little maggot."

"Don't say that," she started angrily. "Maggots are bad...they stink."

"Ahh, but the maggot has a place in this world also. It eats up all the dead flesh so that the germs of the dead cannot be spread all over the countryside. And when the bad smell is gone, then the air is fresh and pure again. I think of you as that...fresh and pure."

Tanya blushed.

"Even the blush that comes to your cheeks reminds me of the sunrise and the sunset. Again the beautiful colors on something so fresh and pure."

That was when he leaned in and kissed her on her

open mouth and she felt his tongue twisting over hers. There was nothing in her that could or would fight off this intruder. She had never had another's tongue stuck in her mouth. There had been some tight-lipped kissing. But those never felt like that first kiss that Gypsy Louie planted on her. At first she thought she'd choke on the heat which seared from his tongue and drifted down into her throat. But she didn't choke and she didn't vomit. Instead the heat quickly centered itself deep in her guts and traveled down the length of her intestines and centered in the rear canal of her vagina. It was such a pleasant heat. She didn't want it to stop, and she knew if she pushed the man away the heat most certainly would stop...the ever so pleasant heat that made her entire pelvic region quiver. A happening that was to carry over throughout her life. Whenever the body heats captured her, her pelvic region would quiver and sometimes even shake, and the heat produced the moisture which rivered down the inside of her thighs. Such a pleasant feeling. And there with Gypsy Louie she knew she wasn't going to let him stop what he was doing. She proved it by pulling him in tightly to her body and the tongues smashed and smashed against each other, and their spit turned hot and they swallowed each other's spit and that felt extra good.

Then his hands were traveling all over the front of her blouse and she felt even better. His lips were locked to hers and his tongue searched the inside of her mouth and his hand went all over her breasts through the material of her blouse. But for the moment he didn't attempt to open the buttons. Instead he kept his left hand in place while the right traveled down the front of her body and then reached up underneath her skirt that he had pulled up for convenience and his hand caressed the crotch of her wet, stained panties. Then his finger searched out the panty leg and he pushed it aside so that he could twirl his finger in her soft pussy hairs. There it remained for what Tanya thought was the longest moment in her life.

But the finger was not satisfied simply playing with the silk-like fur. It started quickly tickling her clitoris and that really was the start of what could only be ended in one way. Then as she really turned on the quivering and the shaking he inserted his finger deep within her. She felt the sudden sharp pain, then the sticky moisture as it came down her leg. But as his finger worked over and over inside the vagina walls, the pain swiftly sped off into eternity. There was no pain left. There was only the pleasure that she wanted and desired, a pleasure she had never experienced when she masturbated herself.

She had heard about men and women from the kids at the school. But no words could explain the feeling that she felt at that moment. There really was something to the whole thing about sex, and men and women getting together for sex after all. But it would never be the same again if she had to diddle herself in the confines of her own room. There would always have to be a man or some second party who would completely take care of her.

Gypsy Louie removed both his hands from their sex attracting position and he bodily lifted her from her feet and took her up in his arms.

"Please don't stop. Not now." Tanya was almost crying in the heat and the pain of wanting.

"Only for a moment. When will your mother or your father be home?"

"Not for all day. They are both at work. Mother just started working, in town, today."

"That's good. Where then is your bedroom at?"

Tanya pointed back along one of the two hails. "Back there...at the back of the hall."

He started carrying her in that direction. "What is your name, little flower?"

"Ruth."

Gypsy Louie thought about that a long time. He thought about her name all the time she sat on the edge of the bed and watched him undress. And he thought about it even longer as he slowly took off her clothing and she stood naked before his very eyes. His eyes became glassy, a demanding glare, and the drool spilled over his thin lips and his handsome features twitched in desire.

"You will no longer be a Ruth to me. You will become Tanya. Tanya...a princess to my tribe! And should you ever meet any of the members of my tribe they will treat you with all the respect due any princess. And I will teach you all the thoughts of the gypsy and what he loves and what he desires, and what he demands of his women. You will be a gypsy princess that will go down in history and you will always know how to service your men." He knelt down and put his lips to her vagina lips. "And you will know what this thing is for, and what men should do to it long before they ever finish up what they must eventually do when they are heated by the woman. And you will learn what makes the woman turn on to what they will like the very best in their thrilling sex life. It is not merely that a man should stick his cock (and he touched his cock) into the girl's cunt (he kissed her cunt). There must be long moments of pure pre-love pleasures when the hands and the tongue and the lips and the nose and the chin must come into action to caress and to love.

"And as the woman she must do the same thing to the man. To have the simple fuck is nothing but spent emotions. The emotions must necessarily be built up to heights before they can be enjoyably spent.

"Do you understand what I am saying, my little Tanya...my little Tanya beauty?"

She nodded her head cautiously. She knew something of what he had said because some of it was told by the boys and the girls at school. But they had never used the flowing terms as Gypsy Louie had spoken, nor did they tell it as romantically and with all the movements his lips and his tongue and his fingers had made upon her body. Tanya was at a point that Gypsy Louie could do anything he wanted with her body...

And he did.

Tanya looked back into the years and over Karl's slashing head, and remembered all that Gypsy Louie had taught her during the two years they were together. He was with her every afternoon in his gypsy wagon in his gypsy camp...every afternoon that her mother and father were away at work. The only time she missed out for their affair was on the two-week vacations and the weekends. But there were many, many days and Tanya learned the world of the sex straights and the sex freaks better than she could ever have learned from any printed book.

It was to stay with her...and it was to make her the head madam at Madam Heles' establishment. And it was to make her the power behind many a man and woman who had left the establishment and gone back into the world with a fuller look at life and their sex problems. Their sex problems had left them. Their only problem was to find mates suitable enough to take on their renewed vigor. But then if they really got hung up on someone who was not up to their standards, there was always Madam Heles' establishment that could teach them the ways of life...and there was always Tanya who could personally service them.

Tanya was proud of her professional knowledge. And she was proud of the majority of her turn outs...or turn ons as the case might be. But there were those in the pit who would never again see the light of day, and those she cried for at times.

She lifted Karl's head and he lay back on the bed, his wet, limp rod drooping between his legs. Tanya bent over it and her ruby red lips encircled the limp shaft and it immediately grew into stiff, rigid life.

8

SHIRLEY STOOD outside of their bedroom door for a long moment. The hallway was dark and as musty as before, and she didn't know quite which way to go as there were many other passage ways along the hall. However, she decided not to go back the way she, Danny and Tanya had come. She was adventurous and always liked to look into the unknown, so why waste time in going back over old trails. Besides, if they were going to see Madam Heles at midnight then undoubtedly they would be going back along that route anyway.

She turned in the opposite direction and the darkness of the hallway increased...and so did the cobwebs. A few times she had to turn her back and brush through them that way so that the filmy material wouldn't get caught in her mouth or her lips. She could always brush the stuff out of her hair later, but in her eyes that could mean scratching, and there was a bitter taste to it when it connected with the taste buds of her tongue. She didn't like that at all.

But it was at one of those turn-arounds when she got the fright of her life. The crack of her fanny, through the thin pink nightie, hit something cold and hard. She gave a jump, startled, and snapped fully around, then her hand went to her mouth to stifle a scream. What came out was only a gasp. But then her eyes narrowed as she searched for the object that had so viciously and unexpectedly attacked her.

A wolf! It was a tremendous wolf that must have weighed more than a hundred pounds. The teeth glistened in the dark in a red-tongued, red-gummed snarl. But there was no sound to the snarl. And there was no sight to the glassy eyes.

The wolf was stuffed.

A taxidermist's perfection.

When she realized what the attack was all about, Shirley

grinned and giggled in her silly manner. She reached out and patted the dry, lifeless hair on the head.

"Good Lord, old fellow, you nearly made me wet my nightie, and it's brand new." Then she realized the presence of someone else in the corridor with her.

The girl was another beautiful object to view. She had the same type of luscious body as Tanya, and she wore the uniform of the house. Only hers was sheer blue, very short and black trimmed. She moved in close to Shirley and laid her hand next to Shirley's on the wolf's head.

"He died of rabies, you know."

"Oh." It was all the beautiful young girl could think of to say. After all, what else was there to say? She was in a hallway with ever-changing shadows that made strange pictures on the walls...any shape her mind apparently wanted them to take. And she was confronted by a stuffed wolf and then there was this lovely, dark-haired creature in sheer blue who brought out words which sounded like musical notes.

The girl let her hand drift across the head of the wolf until it rested over that of Shirley's. Shirley almost pulled it away, but with the light pressure from the girl she felt she'd better let it remain. "You said you were?"

"Barb."

"Barb!"

"Yes."

"Should I know you?"

"You do now, and I know we are going to be excellent friends. All the gils like me...after a while."

"I'm-"

Barb cut her short. "I know."

"You do?"

"We are informed of everyone who comes to visit us. You see, I am one of the inmates also."

"Inmates?"

"Yes! You knowI Like you're in and you can't get out. That kind of inmate."

"We're invited guests."

"Of course you are. And you are most welcome to Madam Heles' establishment. You will be very happy here, I'll see to that. I will so well see to that. And I must say you're a good looking one." She sighed. "There are so many we must service who are not so good looking." She reached over and took Shirley lightly by the back of her neck and pulled her in close. Before Shirley knew what had happened or could do anything about it, Barb had closed her lips over hers and her tongue had been inserted into her mouth.

Shirley got a fiery reaction and pulled away quickly. She didn't quite know what to make of the reaction, but she wasn't about to have some girl kissing her. She quickly remembered Mona and Sally, and thought this could be the same type of thing.

WWhy did you do that?"

"Because I like you."

"Must you be so demonstrative in your liking me?"

"Doesn't everyone kiss when they like each other? I know it to be the most friendly of all gestures."

Shirley thought momentarily that that might have been all there was to the kiss. But if so, why the tongue? However, she cooled and then smiled. She wanted to be friends. After all, perhaps it was also part of the treatment she was to expect and for Danny's sake and to hang on to him, she didn't want to turn down any opportunity of learning...of being cured of her sexlessness. She made the smile much warmer and the girl smiled back.

"You apparently like that!"

Shirley could only answer, "Something happened to me. I must admit that."

"I'm sure it wasn't !like...Danny's."

"You know my husband?"

She nodded. "I have seen him. We have ways, here, of seeing everything that goes on...all who enter and all who stay and all who leave. And we know that you both are so very unhappy."

Shirley clouded. "It is our only problem. Otherwise we enjoy everything life has to offer. Danny is so unhappy...and I am the whole cause."

"Danny will be taken care of." There was a strange note in her words. "When you leave Madam Heles' establishment for the sexually uninformed...the sexually erotically uninformed...you will feel that you have never before lived," She reached down and took both of Shirley's hands in hers. "Do you think you will like me?"

"I feel so strange."

"You are in strange surroundings. It is to be expected. Do you like me?"

"Very much."

"Then trust in me...put your body, your soul, your mind into my hands."

"I've never felt this way before."

"You have never been placed into a position like this before. But it is only a start...just a start, my darling." She let go of one hand and led Shirley back along the corridor to another door through which they entered.

9

DANNY GAVE his usual delivery of the word 'SHIT' then with difficulty slipped back into the red pajama bottoms and said "SHIT" once more then left the gold room. Then on the outside of the bedroom door he encountered much of what Shirley had done before. And he came to the same conclusion she had. He had seen what was behind him, but there was the rest of the hall and all the extra passage ways which led off in other directions. He really wasn't much of an adventurer and never had been during all of his life, even during the two years he spent in the Army. There was a time he found the best shelter and stayed in it and the one thing he could always state as a fact. "At least I got out of the whole thing with a whole ass and not a hole in my ass."

However, except for the strangeness of the house he did have a feeling of security in knowing that the way to the front door was firmly implanted in his mind.

He went in the direction Shirley had gone earlier. And in the same turn-around his rump hit the same dog nose. He made little sound but turned and glared at the long-time dead wolf.

"Your wife was much more demonstrative when she saw the wolf mummy."

Danny didn't snap around that time because the voice of Tanya was quite familiar to him. Then he was looking into her beautiful dark eyes again.

"I was delayed."

"From me...delayed?"

"Yes," then pointedly," Mr. Carpenter."

Danny held his eyes on hers. "Danny's alright...now."

Tanya suddenly lashed out with her right hand and grabbed his prick through the front of the thin red nylon pajama pants. "I've wanted you."

Danny almost ducked back but he couldn't move. Her hand had secured itself through the material and around his prick which shot into motion then stiffly gave her much more room to hold on to.

"What about my wife?" The words were stupid, but as with Shirley previously, there was nothing he could say when he was taken aback with such sudden outward motivations.

"What about her?" Tanya squeezed harder. "Has she ever done this to you?"

"Good Christ no..."

She released his prick and suddenly pulled down his red pajama trousers and his naked, stiff prick was flashed into view. It was then Tanya dropped down quickly arid took it into her mouth. She gave it a couple of licks then stood up again. "Has she ever done that to you?"

"Well...yes...but...not like that."

"Of course not..."

Danny shied a foot or two away from the girl who had gripped his cock tightly again. The foot or two was as far as he could go because of the restraint of her hand.

She made a sexy grin. "Don't you like my hand there on your cock?"

"Well, I...I..." he flustered.

She shoved in closer to him again. "Did you like my lips around it? My hot tongue touching it?"

"Good Christ, you could drive a guy clean out of his skull!"

"Let us hope not that far, Danny. Just far enough so that what happens remains in the grey matter which the skull houses. I will see that you have enough ammunition for all of your thoughts and your illusions. When I do things to you I want your mind to race to the wildest thoughts you can ever imagine. In this way, when perhaps you find another woman who might not be as enjoyable as I shall be, you can transfer all those illusions... and the session will become just as enjoyable as if I were right there." She let her lips ride down along the shaft again. But once more only briefly.

Danny shuddered in expectation. "Good God, and I wondered what we were going to do to pass the time until midnight! Good God!"

Tanya had started to slowly masturbate the young man and she continued the slow, delicious movement that forced Danny to lay back on the gold fur coverlet and open his legs wide so that his shaft stuck straight up toward the ceiling. Tanya stretched cut beside him, but her head was no higher up on the fur coverlet than his crotch line. She would look to his throbbing cock, then up to his eyes, and repeated the eye movement whenever she felt the urge. She also kept up the slow masturbation movements, but it was not a rhythm which was meant to make him pop his nuts. It was simply to keep his mind occupied and him interested until she designed further enjoyments for the affair.

"Would you like to suck my cunt?"

"You know, you talk dirtier than I do."

She spoke softly. "I could use all the medical terms. But would they interest you? Wouldn't you like to hear it as it is? With the words which express everything with no holds barred? Now isn't that better?"

"Don't get me wrong. I wasn't objecting."

"Then, wouldn't you like to suck my cunt?"

"I...I...don't know. I've never done it before."

"Not even to Shirley?"

"She wouldn't hear of such a thing."

"But she sucked you off."

"I forced her into it. Once. There was no completion. She gagged."

"I won't gag."

"And...and...you take it all the way. I mean like all the way and swallow the stuff."

She nodded. "That's the best part...swallowing the cum of your lover. It is like taking a part of him right into the digestive system where the affair lasts so much longer. The girl can know she has it down there for a long time after the explosion has occurred. Ahh, that is by far the very best part of all...taking it down so deep. Feeling the thick juice traveling all the way down your throat. You can feel that going down more than anything else you have ever swallowed. When you eat from my cunt you'll see something of what I mean."

She let go of his cock, gave it a couple of free licks, then came to a kneeling position. She straddled him and with her cunt hairs barely touching his body she traveled all the way up his body until she straddled his face.

She reached down and twiddled her little pea-shaped clitoris. "This is called the little man in the boat. When your tongue hits that you'll send me out of my mind. You'll send me into orbit. Start with that, then let your tongue drift around the lips of my cunt, then dig your tongue deep inside of me, deep in where all the sweet juices of life are stored. You'll make me cum this way, then I'll favor you and your dreams will be answered."

Danny gripped the cheeks of her ass and drove his lips tight against the lips of her vagina, and his tongue slashed back and forth, then around, then sunk into the vagina as far as he could. He liked what he felt and he liked what he tasted, and when her pubic region started to gyrate slowly above he liked that even more. He could feel the shocks leaving her body and entering his own, and they exploded down in his balls and stiff cock until the purple head was throbbing for some kind of acceptance.

"Good God," he moaned into her cunt. "Good God, I never knew it could feel like this."

Tanya didn't answer. She began to moan and her body swayed suddenly, wildly from side to side until Danny felt her whole body go rigid, then spent, then rigid again, then spent and she climaxed seven times before she finally was satisfied and she relaxed. Slowly she let him out of the saddle and she stretched out beside him on the bed. Then she rolled her head so that she faced him and she kissed him full on the open lips. "I like to taste my own stuff also."

"God, you got a crazy cunt."

"I'm glad you liked it."

Both his hands were holding his throbbing prick. "But I'm hot as hell. I got to come off. When do you take care of me?"

"Now," she said simply, then reached to the side of the bed and lifted up the gigantic dildo. She squeezed the rubber-like testicles and the high pitched sound was transferred elsewhere in the house. But it was only a moment until another girl, one Danny had not seen before, entered the room. Along with high heeled shoes she only wore skimpy fur panties and a brassiere-like halter.

Danny was amazed. "What's she for?"

"Servicing." Tanya sat up on the edge of the bed. "He will eat you, and I will do the rest. Keep the fur brassiere on and we will see how the fur affects his fetish talents."

The new girl removed her fur panties and dropped them on the side of the bed, then she assumed the position over his face as Tanya had previously done. If Danny had had a hard on before, it was twice as powerful at that point. He moaned into the girl's cunt. He wanted to speak, to cry out, but all he could muster up were the delighted groans.

Tanya waited until she heard his tongue slapping against the girl's vagina lips, then she stretched back across the bed and took his throbbing dork into her mouth. She made one lick and he was spurting jism with the force of a stud horse. Tanya gulped it down, but then she came off the prick with complete disgust written all across her face, although Danny couldn't see it, he was too deep in the new girl's muff.

"That will never do," she said, then roughly pulled the new girl from Danny's face. "Leave us, Delilah."

Delilah slipped off the edge of the bed and sexily pulled on her panties, then still wordlessly left the room.

"You're too much. You know that, Danny? You really are too much."

Still amazed at the turn of events, Danny pushed up his body and held it there with his elbows on the bed.

"Now what in hell did you go and do that for? I was just getting started on her. She's got one hell of a box. Maybe not as active as yours, Tanya, but one hell of a fur-box anyway."

Tanya shook her head sadly. "You'll never please any girl that way."

"What...by eating her box? You said it was important. At least you led me to believe that."

"Of course, cunt licking is important. it's all part of the build-up. but that's not what I'm talking about.
"

"Then what the hell are you talking about?"

"Do you know how long it took you to pop your nuts that time."

"Right quick." He grinned, and the words were those of a braggart.

"Wipe that God damned smile off your face. That's not something to be proud of."

"I've always shot off quick."

"That's your problem!"

"I don't see where it's any problem,"

"What do you think you do to the girl?"

"She gets the load."

"And that's about all she gets. You come off like that, you don't give a girl a chance to enjoy herself, let alone get worked up to a climax. A broad tangles with you and that dick will always find herself finger fucking herself or using one of these things." She held up the alarm clock, then put it back as he spoke.

"I don't get you."

"Just because you spit out your cum doesn't mean that the girl has cracked her nuts. No girl can get to a climax that fast. You hit your load, you get the good feeling then forget all about that you haven't in the least taken care of the girl. You've left her with a hot cunt and nothing to put out the fire."

"I always thought...that...well, when a guy comes so does the girl. They bounce like they do."

"You wouldn't know if they bounced or not. You're too worked up in your own pleasures. Have you ever asked them if they were satisfied?"

"I don't remember any complaints."

"Ahh, but do you remember many of them coming back for a second try?"

Danny didn't say anything, but his mind drifted back to one special occasion. The girl's name was Marsha, and she had hair as black as a raven, and her pussy hair had also matched. Damn, how he wanted her! He wanted her so bad that every time he looked at her he was mentally undressing her. It was during their junior year in high school and she had the seat opposite him. She was another one like Shirley who loved sweaters, and because her youthful body was fully developed by the time she was sixteen, she looked like the real sweater girl. His mental pictures, however, always saw her completely undressed sitting there at her desk. Many times during that period he had been reprimanded for not looking to his lessons. But scolding by the teacher or not, he couldn't keep his eyes off Marsha nor could he keep his penis from rising in his shorts...an entity which would have caused him much embarrassment if at those times he'd been called upon to stand up. But the teachers didn't take his nonsense very long. And they were no dummies. They knew just about what the score was. And they changed his seat. It was better to give him a little embarrassment than the girl. After all, she wasn't caught looking at him.

But she had been. And that same afternoon when

they got out of class she told him about her own feelings. And it didn't take them long to realize that his prick was throbbing and her cunt was twitching beneath her pink skirt. She was wearing a pink skirt and a pink mohair cardigan, extremely bulky, due to the cold weather, but it did little to hide her exquisite body.

They knew what they wanted from the moment they kissed in an alley they traveled on their way home. And in the closeness of the kiss Danny's rod, still encased in his trousers, attempted to cut through the skirt and into her golden hole. She had pulled away from him slightly, but kept her arms around his strong waist.

"Not here. God, not here...but someplace." She was breathing heavily.

"I know. I know. I got to have you. God, you do things to me. You do things like no other girl has ever done." He could hardly keep from shooting his load into his shorts.

"You must know of some place?"

"Sure...sure." He produced a key. "I got a key to the side door of the theatre. I work there on weekends. It's all ours for the taking. Nobody's there until seven."

"Let's hurry." She gripped his arm and they nearly ran the distance to the theatre.

Danny was shaking all over by the time they reached the side door to the State Theatre where Danny was a weekend usher, and Marsha wasn't any better. Every so often she had to press her hand hard to the front of her skirt as if the move and the pressure would still her wanting pangs. But then it was open, and he took her hand to lead her through the darkness to the ladies' room where the only lounge was located.

Then, once secure behind the locked door, he turned on a small light and took her in his arms. The fuzzy mohair sweater was soft to his touch and each fibre seemed to have its own electrical charge which heightened his sexual needs. He tongue lashed her and she returned with the same fire. Her hands dropped, both of them, to take his enormous dork through the pants front. He might have continued to feel her beautiful titties through the sweater for a lot longer time because he realized she was wearing no brassiere. But Marsha was hot and ready. Her groin ached for release. The sweat had already started to river its way down the inside of her legs, and the heat from her body started to boil the water at the crotch of her panties. The time was ripe. She wanted that long prick inside of her and she wanted it there a long time. She knew she could have at least six or eight climaxes during any one affair.

She dreamed of each one in turn as she said, "Now, baby, now! Don't even take time to undress. Just drop your pants and dig that thing into me. Give it to me hard and terrifying. Shoot me full of your jism. Tie up my stomach in knots." She dropped down to the flowered couch and pulled up her skirt and pulled off her panties while Danny unbuckled his pants and let them drop to the floor around his ankles. He kicked them free. "Get on to me...get on to me. Stick in in. Stick it in deep! Take a long time in there. Danny, stick it in!" Her hand fought to grab his dick. His hands pushed the sweater up around her neck without even attempting to unbutton it. Her beautiful tits popped into sight and with a moan he attacked each of them with his lips and his tongue.

She gripped his dick with all her might and forced it through the lips of her vagina, and with a hefty shove from his ass he sent the dick in to the hilt, and he also shot his load on the thrust...then the meat died to the limp state and he was done.

"You fuckin' God damn cocksucker. You bastard! You fuckin' quickie shit head. You lousy cuntsucker. You miserable scum of the earth!" she pushed him hard away and he rolled to the floor as she spread her legs and inserted her own finger. All the time she leveled curses at him until suddenly she screamed once and her little ass pounded up and down heavily on the divan. Then with each of her spurts her body stiffened, relaxed, then stiffened again.

Finally she was finished, but not satisfied. She pushed her legs over the edge of the lounge, grabbed up her panties and pulled them on angrily. "Don't you ever speak to me again!" she screamed and ran for the door.

Danny looked at Tanya. "I've had my troubles."

"I can bet you have..." Tanya frowned deeply. "You are going to be a tough one...but there's a way of fixing you. I'm sure of that. In the meantime let's try that thing on for size once more."

She bent down and took the soft shaft full into her rnouth, taking his balls also in her hand and gently massaging them.

10

SHIRLEY FOUND herself in a strange position. It was like she was once more witnessing the action of Mona and Sally. The names perhaps were different, but the same actions were involved, only more intense...involved...perhaps more professional...more know-how in the entire approach to the affair.

When Barb had brought her so gently into the blue room Shirley hadn't known quite what to expect. The room was so under-lit she could only see strange shadows and shapes. It was obvious, however, that each of the shadows and the shapes were female in form. But in understanding what the moving shapes were, she couldn't help but wonder what the faces looked like, or what the whole thing was going to culminate in.

For the moment the entire atmosphere was like the dance of reptiles in a snake pit. It was the only illusion behind her conscious thoughts.

But Shirley was not going to be permitted to stay in the dark very long.

Barb snapped her fingers and with that signal command the room slowly lightened to a ghostly blue, but one that lighted up the figures so that the entire forms could be seen...in variations of blue...faces, negligees, bodies...variations of blue.

Barb squeezed Shirley's hand and then she led her to the opposite side of the room...to a blue, throne-like affair. Barb put her into the seat then backed off.

"From here you will witness everything there is to see!" Barb grinned and Shirley attempted to decipher the grin as evil or sexy...the blue lights fogged her thinking brain, her conception of what she was seeing as an illusion thereof. She could only wonder with fascinated eyes as Barb said simply, "Watch!"

She watched. Her deep blue eyes could do nothing but watch. Blue filtering through blue settled all the other issues. The cloud of the imagination put her at ease...a restful ease which opened her eyes, yet captured her spirit and her will to move.

"Drink this!" It was Barb's smooth, delicate musical voice that accompanied the hand and the silver goblet.

Shirley took the mixture...sweet...almost a sickly sweet...sticky. She drank it down. It burned all the way to her stomach, but then the burning turned to a pleasant heat, and as a finale she felt a feeling of complete tranquillity steal through her. She was at complete peace with the world. At another time she might have objected to what was about to happen all around her, but there and then she was strapped to the throne chair without the aid of straps or chains. Her entire inner being was held by invisible hands and she found herself not really wanting to move.

"Can you understand what I say?" Barb's voice had lost none of the musical tones.

"Yes!" Shirley felt her word come out as if it were all

dreamy...as if it traveled from some far-off distance, then floated out in front of her.

"That is good. All you must do is relax and you will see and you will learn."

"Yes. See...relax."

Barb turned to the first of the girls and took her by the hand. She brought her in close to her and their eyes studied each other for a long moment, then as if neither of them had taken the first step or made the first movement, their arms went around each other and with their hands continually in motion over their bodies, their lips met, and Shirley could hear the soft moaning sounds coming from the spacelessness between their tightly pressed lips. Then she could even hear the soft sounds of their wet, pink tongues as they searched through the caverns that were their mouths.

Then the hands came around to the front and four hands found four breasts through the sheer material of the negligee. They fondled each other that way for a long time until Barb once more took a step backward and her dainty hands went to the tie ribbons at the shoulders of the lovely girl. The ribbons came apart easily...with little or no force. But Barb didn't let the soft garment fall immediately to the floor. Instead she clasped it just beneath the breast of the girl and held it there while she knelt down to encircle only the nipple of the girl's right breast. She licked it with her tongue until little rivulets of saliva drained over the mound.

She moved her head to the left breast and did the same, and to Shirley it seemed Barb lingered there the longest before she moved her head again and took the entire globe of the right breast into her mouth. The girl receiving the action threw back her head and squeals of delight issued from her mouth. Then her hand flew down between her own legs. She pulled up the hem of the negligee and quickly inserted her finger into her cunt. She worked furiously in and out of the juicy box and lingered many times on her clitoris, working at it furiously. Her thighs started slowly back and forth and gyrating. Then as the heat produced itself more intensely in her body, the movements became as violent as the movement of her finger.

She raised up on her tiptoes forcing her front out and as far and as close to Barb as possible. Barb remained with the globe in her mouth, sucking furiously. First one then the other. Then she dropped her own hand down to the girl's cunt, and inserted her own finger into the wet box along with the girl's. Both fingers worked as one, and the girl's squeals turned to screams of pain and delight at the same time.

Bending low into the tit, Barb reached around the girl's body with her free left hand and inserted her index finger deep into the other's anus. This really made the girl go into spewing jerks of ecstasy.

Then, with one last deep plunge, the girl flung herself away from Barb. She fell to a blue fur rug where her body rose and fell in her climax, and another girl drifted down on top of her to bury her face deep into the pubic region, her tongue lashing wildly as the body juices pumped and spilled, pumped and spilled, over and over again. And the second girl lifted her own shortie nightie and did the firmer insertion bit.

"Mary," commanded Barb softly as a pretty redhead came to her.

Mary held an enormous dildo in her hand which she handed to Barb for inspection.

"Is it filled?"

"Yes...very warm and perfumed."

"Good." Then Barb handed it back to Mary. "Strap it into place."

The girl lifted her shortie nightie up over her head and then let the filmy material drift to the floor at her feet. She stepped into the braces of the dildo straps and pulled it up around her ass so that the cock-like affair was perfectly adjusted to that spot over her pussy where a man's dick would be. She tied the rest of the straps behind her for complete security.

Barb snapped her fingers in the direction of a long-haired blonde. "Lana." The blonde drifted in to face her. "Assume the position."

The beautiful blonde Lana knelt down on all fours with her rump held high. She pulled her pink negligee up along her back until it hung free from around her neck. The rest of her body was naked and exposed. Mary took the gigantic dildo in both hands and led it to the mark, right at Lana's pussy opening. She held it there poised for a long moment, then shoved it home with all her might. Lana gave one painful shout, then drifted off into the ecstasy of feeling...a sound which could only shout as to how much she enjoyed what was happening to her.

She let one of her hands drift back to the instrument and she held it on all the outward pulls so that it would immediately go back in, straight and true to the mark. Her eyes opened and closed with each thrust and pull out. Her breasts bobbed underneath her, and her breath became tight, and she gritted her teeth to keep from blowing off too soon. Barb didn't like it when any of her girls came off too soon.

Barb really did like to watch. All of her life she could remember liking the voyeuristic views on sex. That's why she so much enjoyed her work with Madam

Heles. She never put the new client into the act immediately. She would have her, as Shirley was doing, sit on the throne for several prolonged sessions before she ordered her to participate. But that would be in the future. Shirley was not ready. Barb felt she had a difficult client on her hands. But all in good time. And the narcotic she had slipped into Shirley's drink was working wonders...the girl simply sat there, wide-eyed...fascinated.

And Barb knew the size of the dildo going into Lana's ass wasn't hurting the girl a bit. She had taken it and larger ones many times before, But if Shirley hadn't been mentally fogged she would have been almost feeling pain herself. In voyeuristic delights sometimes pain as well as pleasure could be transferred.

Barb had learned to turn on whatever she wanted from the sight. She was a master at transference to her own brain.

———

ONCE SHE HAD SEEN a beautiful drag queen raped by six men in an alley. It was a sight of pure terror because they ripped the young boy's ass right out. The blood and the gore was a horrible sight to witness. But after the initial pain shot through her voyeuristic eyes she felt pleasure in all they did to him.

That night Barb had felt something was going to happen. It wasn't a pleasant bar the guy she had picked up had taken her to. It was a waterfront type of bar, but was situated far from any waterfront. It was a dimly lighted place which undoubtedly had had trouble in obtaining any kind of a liquor license. But evidently it had, because there was not only the usual beer and wine served in such places, but also the hard liquor. And, if the stuff was wanted, there was no doubt that anybody could capture all the dope and varieties of dope they wanted. But as she whored the street she never knew where her 'John' was going to take her. This would undoubtedly be a lay in the back room of the saloon.

She remembered saying to herself. "This creep is so cheap he won't even lay out for a sleazy motel or hotel room. Another one of those bastards with a cot in the back of a saloon...and ten to one he'll invite half a dozen of his crummy friends to have me too. Well, they better lay out the dough." This was long before she had made the connections whereby she could really get the clientele with the big money...and the eventual introduction to Madam Heles and her perfect set-up.

The guy bought several cocktails for her which made her feel a little better about being with the creep. She liked martinis and what they did for her. And it was while she was on number five that the door opened and he came in. She knew him from the street. He was a male whore and he dressed in girl's clothes. His stock in trade were the big studs who wanted the thrill of a homosexual outing for a night and for the homosexuals who were in the difficult position of having to keep their true identity and demands secret. Undoubtedly, that night, he was to meet someone at the bar, otherwise he wouldn't have chanced such a place.

Sandra, which was what he called himself, wore the same outfit he always wore. Long, more than shoulder length, blonde hair over a long sleeved red mohair cardigan, buttoned down the front, white skirt and red high-heeled shoes. Barb could visualize also the pink brassiere, pink panties and pink mini slip underneath.

She'd seen him in action in the alleys many times and knew that was what he always wore.

But she was to see him in action that night as she had never realized was possible that anyone could live through.

And it was her 'John' who started the whole thing. "Well, if it ain't our little queer boy."

"Let him alone, Phil," Barb groaned, knowing what was about to happen because of the amount of liquor Phil (her 'John') had consumed.

"Shit, the little faggot wants to get fucked. I think he should get fucked."

"You got me."

"I can get you any time."

And those around them in the bar who could hear turned over with belly laughs. "Why don't you prick him, Phil?" shouted a female tramp of the dollar-a-night kind.

"Sure, let's see what kind of a cunt he's got!" Another voice touted.

"You jab him in the ass-cunt and he can suck me at the same time."

"How's for a gang bang?"

Sandra smoothed out the fur of the red sweater and realized he was in for trouble. No 'John' in a bar was worth waiting for when the odds were all wrong.

He had started to sit up at the bar stool, but uncrossed his dainty legs and stood back on the floor. "Is Terry here?" he asked in the falsetto voice.

"Ain't no Terry," laughed the old hag in the corner. "But how about me, honey, I can give you a dose of clap easier than any prick." And she cackled with the others joining in.

Sandra kept his eyes on the others as he backed to

the door. He wasn't about to turn his back on anybody. But that wasn't good enough. He backed into a guy named Grundy who had locked the door and stood in front of it.

Grundy directed his words to the bartender as Sandra, frightened out of his wits, turned to look into the evil face, the tobacco stained slimy lips. "We're gonna use your back room awhile, Harry."

"Cost you three bucks like always."

"Fair enough at double the price." Then he reached out and grabbed the red sweater-covered arms.

Sandra squealed and might have screamed, but another dirty man came up behind him and lamped a filthy hand over his mouth. Then two more men jumped into the scene and grabbed Sandra's legs and flailing arms. Sandra tried to kick with the spike heels and claw with the long nails, but it was like a fly attacking the thick skin of an elephant. He was dragged off into the back room amid the cheers of the others in the room. Phil hopped off the bar stool next to Barb, and taking her by the arm, pulled her across toward the back room with him.

"Come on, you're gonna like what you see." He pulled her into the back room and a sixth man followed close at their heels.

Barb knew there was no use in attempting to escape what she was going to see. All she'd end up with, in not doing Phil's bidding, would be a black eye, maybe some broken teeth or a broken arm.

"Strip the maggot naked," yelled the one called Grundy.

"Hell no, you idiot," shouted Phil. "That wouldn't be no more than fuckin' anybody in the ass. Keep the girl's clothes on him and you get to keep the illusion.

And if his dork and bails hang down too low we'll cut them off."

Sandra screamed at the thought and a hand went over his red lipstick-painted mouth which was badly smeared from all the hand treatment during the past few minutes.

"Just get the panties off the drag queen. That's all you got to take off."

Sandra was lifted off the floor again and the panties quickly removed and shoved into his mouth.

"Let's try the swinging back door," shouted Phil and it was more of a demand than a request.

Two men took his right and left arm and another two lifted him off the ground, one on each of his legs. He was spread apart, and Phil took his hard dong out through the open zipper of his pants and moved into position. He looked down at the boy's balls and prick so limp, hanging low in front of him, and Phil knew what he was going to do before that night was over. Then, as the men spread the legs as far apart as they could without tearing him in quarters, Phil jammed his prick home. The sobs and the moans and the muffled scream forced their way through the thick glob of panties which was secured in his mouth. The tears of pain and humiliation welled up in Sandra's eyes and he spilled them all down his cheeks. But there were no tears that could turn these men off. Each could feel the swelling of their own cocks and each would soon be demanding the next attack.

Phil was built big, and he took Sandra with such force that he ruptured something on only the second thrust and a gush of blood came drooling out of Sandra's ass. But the blood could just as well have been more tears. Phil shoved it home time and time again until he felt all the pressure building up inside of himself. He grabbed the boy's ass with one hand and his hanging prick and balls with the other, and when he shot his load deep into the boy's guts he yanked the boy's balls until he felt they would come off.

Then the first one was over and Phil took his place in holding up one of the legs while the next man stepped into the deep "V" and shoved his shaft home.

Sandra hurt bad by this time. He'd taken it in the ass many times since he'd become a drag queen whore of the street...but never with such viciousness. When he charged for his services he expected some roughness. But there was nothing equal to the terror of a bunch of drunken slobs with lust and torture on their minds. They were going to tear him apart and he knew it, and there was nothing in this world he could do about it except hope that he'd live through the ordeal and it wouldn't take him too long to heal up. He had to keep working. It was the only way he had of making a buck.

And stranger still were Sandra's thoughts as he was taken by the fourth of the pack. The pain had so increased that he wished he could black out, but he couldn't...but there was some kind of a comfort in that the pain brought on crazy thoughts...like he hoped the blood wasn't getting all over the white skirt. Naturally it was, he knew that, and he knew it would be ruined. And he knew the expensive fuzzy, soft red mohair cardigan had been torn at the sleeve hem, and the filth of their dirty and bloody hands could never again be cleaned from it. It would be a total loss.

And he didn't even know it, or feel it when Phil took out his eight inch switchblade knife, as sharp as any razor and severed his cock and balls, and shoved the cock head in to replace the sopping panties. That was when the lights really went out for the boy...the black lights with only lightning streaks which flashed behind his mind's eye. It would be many hours before he knew what had happened.

But Barb remembered, and she remembered him as he later went in for the sex change. Phil didn't know, at the time, what he was really doing for the mixed-up lad who would soon be all woman...

———

BARB WATCHED Shirley's eyes as the dildo was taken out of Lana, squirting the warm, white perfumed liquid which looked and felt so much like cum. She watched and she would watch more as the night wore on. Barb appreciated watching more than any other person she'd ever come in contact with.

11

DANNY HELD HIS WET, slippery dick in his hands as he looked at the frowning Tanya. He had done it again. She got him all worked up with her tongue and those hot, wet lips, and he shot into her mouth before she had sucked it three strokes. The cum was still drooling through the corners of her lips. She had been too angry to even bother wiping it off.

"That's the third time," she gobbled and the stuff drooled out even faster.

"I tried, honestly I tried."

"I can understand...I'm about the best cock sucker in the world. But this is ridiculous."

"The same thing happens when I put it in your cunt. I get so hot I just gotta let go."

"You really are a poor soul."

"Well, anyway it feels good. That's what it's supposed to do...feel good, isn't it?"

"Feel good for who?"

"I mean it felt good to me...all three times." He blinked, "Does that mean you're going to quit me...give me up as a bad job?"

"We have never given anyone up. But I do believe I'm going to try you out with one of the other girls. Doris might be an interesting one for you. She's a masochist. You can beat hell out of her with anything you want and she'll cry her way all the way through the affair."

"I don't know if I'd like that...beating up on a woman. That's never been anything I like to do."

"You're going to try everything while you're here, and I mean everything. it's the only way we're going to find out what's best for you."

"I've been this way so long I doubt if anything is ever going to change me."

"Oh, something will present itself." She reached down into the night stand beside the bed and brought out a towel that she generously applied to her mouth, wiping the cum away. "But you sure do have sweet cum."

"Something different than other men?"

"Some have sweet cum some have sour, some have salty stuff and still others doctor it all up by soaking the head of their prick in all kinds of things."

"Is that ethical?"

"Ethical, hell. Anything that turns a guy or a gal on is ethical. Sex is for pleasure and whatever gives the most pleasure, then that's the right step."

"Do women do that to their pussy too?"

"Of course. At least the modern girl does. There are all sorts of sprays for the pussy. Chocolate, vanilla, lemon, grape, spices. You name it and some supplier of such things can supply them. We've got them all right here in our store room. We'll try you out on some. What flavor would you like to start with?"

"Anything but chocolate. "

"I favor strawberry."

Danny laughed heartily. The whole situation started to sound completely silly to him. "Then by all means let's dip my cock in strawberry. Since you're going to be eating it, you might just as well eat something you like." Then he laughed again.

"Sex and what makes somebody happy is no laughing matter." Tanya narrowed her eyes.

"Maybe not sex itself. But this situation is wild."

"Glad you're enjoying YOURSELF."

"Oh, I am...I am." He wiggled his dick with both hands.

"But l don't think this thing is going to be ready for some time yet. I'm not used to such prolonged, numerous sessions."

"You will be hardened to the life."

"I'm not sure I want to. You'll have this thing so raw I won't be able to put my shorts on."

"You won't need any until you're cured."

"Say, what's all this cured about? It's Shirley who needs the curing. She's the reason we're here."

Tanya smiled knowingly, but she covered his remark only with, "Of course. That's the reason." Then she slid off the bed and picked up the giant dildo which she pressed and moments later a lovely girl in a long black nightgown trimmed with black marabou, entered the room. "This is Doris."

"S0 this is Doris."

"She will get you ready for anything."

"Nobody's going to beat me."

"I told you before. Doris is a masochist. She is not a sadist who does the beatings. That will be your role in the affair." She reached over and pressed a hidden switch. A large paneling in the wall beside Denny's portion of the bed opened.

Inside were a great assortment of cat-o'-nine-tails, whips, belts and other implements of torture. His eyes bugged at the assortment.

"Perhaps through your exercise you will find something that can give you cause to harden up, and to be able to restrain shooting off. The process will come from somewhere and we must continue until it is found with whatever is necessary."

Danny surveyed the beautiful blonde in the black marabou trimmed nightgown. "One thing for damned sure. You've got the most beautiful dolls in this house that I've ever seen."

"We house only the very best that money can buy. That's why our bill is so high."

"You would have to mention the bill."

"Money, like sex, can be the root of all evil. But it can also be the root of all worldly pleasures." Then she silently turned away and moved to a gold fur-covered chair and sank into the deep, soft luxury of it. She made a quick glance to Doris.

Doris faced Danny directly. "Would you like me naked or would you prefer ripping the nightdress from my luscious body?"

"Proud of yourself, aren't you."

"We must all be proud of ourselves."

"Take the nightie off," he said, reaching up for the cat-o'-nine-tails. "I'd hate to think of ruining something as pretty as that garment."

"Perhaps you would like to put it on?"

"What?" Danny was really startled.

"Many men would like to put something like this on."

"Fruit cakes."

"Not all of them."

"Real he-type men wouldn't be caught dead in something like that."

"Not dead. But very much alive. We have many clients who prefer fucking while wearing ladies' garments, especially nighties. Do not women often times wear pajamas?"

"That's different."

"On the contrary...not different at all...in most cases. People have so many, so varied, so interesting ways of preparing themselves for the action of sex."

"Like you and your whips?"

"Of course." She hugged her arms around her as if she were already feeling the sting of the whips and the anticipation of the action thrilled her. She always felt the heat deep within her pussy first, but she also knew it would travel swiftly up into her brain and there it would stay until the whips and the belts started to attack her skin.

She likes to remember her first experience. Most people like to remember the first experience in anything they did which brought them some kind of pleasure. Her pleasure had come through the beating that a man dealt her because she had been a virgin.

Doris had found herself in a strange town after she ran away from home. But more than a strange and seemingly unfriendly town, but she was broke and had no place to stay and she was hungry. She didn't know what it was like to be a whore, a street walking whore, but she knew what the words meant and she knew what she would have to do if she found a guy who would take her.

She was sixteen, but she looked eighteen, and she

had thwarted off the prying hands of many a boy during her school years. Oh, some of them got so far as to put their hands on the front of and up under her blouse or her sweaters, and most of them were permitted the usual kissing...that's where she learned what tongue or French kissing was all about. But none of them had ever gotten into her panties. In fact none of them had even gotten so far as to see what color of panties they were or what material they were made out of. She was one hundred percent virgin lust like when she was born.

But most men liked virgins. She didn't feel that would be any problem. Perhaps the men who would pay for her open leg services might have wanted somebody more experienced. But there was only one way of getting experienced, and that was by doing. And, broke and alone in a strange town, and hungry...there was no time like the present to get started.

She shouldn't have any trouble, All men liked new young stuff.

She selected a sheer white blouse and put on a black satin brassiere underneath so that the entire outline would show through. Men like to see things like that. It was really a very sexy sight. And she smoothed an extremely short brown mini skirt over her hips. She didn't wear stockings and she didn't own any high heels, but the white boots, she thought, were sexy as all get out. Boots also did a lot for turning a guy on.

They turned a guy named Wilson on.

He eyed her up and down as she slowly passed him on the afternoon street. She had thought of waiting until after dark, but her stomach growls wouldn't permit any more waste of time. He looked her over, then stopped her with a stupid question.

"Do you have a light?"

There was no doubt in her mind that the man had money. She knew an expensive suit when she saw one. "I don't smoke."

"Some people carry matches even if they don't smoke."

"I don't."

"The line was only to stop you anyway."

"I know." She smiled broadly.

"Would you like a cocktail with me?"

"Bars won't serve me. I'm only eighteen." She lied about her age. But who could really tell. She had the tittie work of at least that age and her eyes sparkled enough to cover such a small white lie.

"My apartment is quite near here, I wouldn't ask you for your identification card."

"Do you know how to make a martini?"

"Are martinis what you like?"

"I don't know, I've never had one."

He pondered that a moment. "I suppose that has some deep underlying meaning."

"I've often read about martinis. I suppose I should try one when I get the chance. Do you know how to make them?"

"The easiest cocktail to mix in the world."

She looped her arm through his and she didn't care who saw her do it. They met on the street. She a woman, and he a man. Who was to say they hadn't been friends for years? And the man, Wilson, he introduced himself as soon as they started walking, wasn't kidding her when she said his apartment was quite near. It was in the middle of the same block where they had met. And the building was one of the more exclusive mansion type apartment houses on the row. And his own apartment was a lavish affair, done in deep colors.

The furniture was expensive and ornate in design, and as he showed her around the entire apartment he casually opened the bedroom door and she saw the same deep tones in color, but the room was entirely done in velvet materials. Velvet on the bed, the drapes and the furniture. She would learn later that the drapes pulled back to reveal the entire room was encircled with mirrors.

But for the moment he sat her down, then went to a fancy bar where all the mixings were and he mixed a large container full of the clear liquid.

"Looks like water," she opinioned, as he handed her the crystal cocktail glass.

"Well, it will hit the bottom of your tummy a lot harder and hotter than any water you've ever drank."

She liked the mixture. She liked it to the tune of four more, and marveled as her eyes fogged and cleared. "Maybe I'd better lay down for awhile," she cooed over the delightful sensation.

"Isn't that why you're here...to lie down?"

"Yes...yes, I suppose so. But I do feel a little dizzy right n0w."

"You'll be fine in a little while." He led her across to the bedroom and left her just inside the doorway while he went back to get the shaker full of martinis. He put it on a silver service tray near the bed, then came back lo take her arm and lead her to the bed. She sat down on the edge. "You'll feel a lot better if you take your clothes off."

Doris knew that she would have to sooner or later. It was what she had planned on, But the martinis on such an empty stomach were more than she could bear. She thought perhaps she could lay her legs open to him for one time, then ask for something to eat. She didn't think he'd be happy if he were put off before he got it at least once.

She stood up and reached for the buttons on the back of her blouse, but Wilson stepped in and did the honors. Then he lowered his hands and slid down the zipper on the back of her skirt. She was then revealed only in panties and brassiere, and some of her cunt hairs stuck down through the leg of her panties. Another time she might have been embarrassed at such a thing. But the martinis had taken their toll, and she didn't care one way or another if the cunt hairs showed or not. And a moment later all her cunt hairs were showing because Wilson stripped the panties from her body right after he had unfastened the brassiere, and she moved her arms so that it would fall freely down from her arms and land on the floor. The panties joined the brassiere on the floor and she laid back and opened her legs.

"Will it hurt?"

Her words took the man aback. He was standing over her naked, and with his enormous cock in his right hand. He wasn't even going to give her any pre-love action. There wasn't going to be any kissing or tittie-feeling like all the boys liked to do. He was simply going to shove it into her pussy and have at it. "Will what hurt?" he asked in amazement, then looked to his cock, then back to her pussy again. "Will what hurt?"

She indicated his cock. "That. Will it hurt when you stick that big cock into me."

"Don't you know?"

She shook her head. "I've never had a cock in me before. I've played with myself, with my finger. But no man has ever been with me...no man has ever shoved a cock into me."

"A fuckin' virgin! Good Christ, I got a fuckin' virgin!" Then he slapped her across the face. Again and again both his hands went back and forth across her face, her body, her tits, her pussy, the rump of her ass when she turned over, attempting unsuccessfully to get away from him.

Then all of a sudden she didn't want to get away from him. In one of his fast moves he had pulled a bell type cord and the drapes fell away to reveal all the mirrors. He had suddenly started watching what he was doing in the mirror and the lust for what he was doing showed heavily in his eyes. He panted and the breathing came strong through his chest, and he beat harder and harder. He reached over the bed and picked up the belt. He wrapped the buckle around his hand and beat the hell out of her tits, then spun her over and brought welt after welt across her lovely little rump. And that's when the strange sensation started going through her body. The stinging belt no longer hurt. The stinging seemed to transfer itself into heat patches which turned on every nerve in her body. She began to twitch. The heat in her mouth caused the saliva to run from the corner of her eyes. The lust in her own eyes suddenly matched the lust in his eyes. She started to scream, but it was not the screams of pain. She was screaming for more...ever more.

"Beat me, damn it...beat me...cut me up...hit my tits. Beat hell out of me. Swing that belt until your arm falls off, then ram that big cock deep inside of me." Her own hands went to her tits and she squeezed them over and over again. She tried to hurt them, but there was no pain, only the pleasure and the fire which seared up inside of her cunt as she rolled over and over on the bed, ever toward the whip, and when the man's emotions became so pent up that he had to break or go mad he fell to the front of her and jammed his cock into her as hard as he could.

The cherry broke and the blood and slime shot all over both their fronts. But he took her with the fury of a man gone mad with the sex lust. He had hurt her when the cherry broke and Doris knew he was still hurting her, but there was no hurt. All she felt was pleasure and what was building up inside of her. The heat was terrifying, but she could only wish it were a real fire that was being forced through her body. She wanted the searing pain of the flame...but the heat of sex is all too soon gone...and it left her in six sudden rushes of her own climaxes and she felt him shoot his hot jism all over the inside walls of her cunt. But it took a long time for him to quit pumping, and she didn't stop her own shooting until he sunk, exhausted, to the bed beside her.

———

"YOU'RE sure you want it this way?" questioned Danny as he raised the cat-o'-nine-tails for a last inspection.

"It's the only way, honey," breathed Doris. She was getting hotter and hotter by the moment. The anticipation was a fire ball to her mental structure.

And as he got to his knees she reached down and took up the marabou hemline and pulled the nightie up over her head, and when it was clear she held it out as if to him.

"Are you sure you don't want to wear this?"

He cracked her with all his might and she fell screaming to the bed where she would roll around under his swing for more than an hour while Tanya masturbated herself across the room.

12

DANNY WATCHED the girl limp out of the room lugging her black, marabou trimmed nightgown with her. She had been had with the whip and she had climaxed over and over again...and when it had been time for her to scream for Danny to take her, to shove it in deep, to take her with all his male strength, all his manly manhood, his stiff shaft, his large purple head, the cock not of his choosing, but he was stuck with it, he tackled the aching cunt the same as he had always done.

With one hand he found the hole, with the other he guided the arrow toward the target and with his strong ass he plunged the dart inward and by the time the purple head hit the outer lips, the first set of lips just below the clitoris he was shooting all over her pubic hairs. The cum went nowhere except down the lips of Doris' cunt and circled into sticky spots on the gold sheets...the gold fur coverlet had been removed simply because of what was thought might happen. A thought which came true. He was once more spilling his load where it will do no good.

Tanya had watched and thoroughly enjoyed herself.

But she frowned as she watched the door close behind Doris. But at least she had completed the come off of her own jollies in perhaps not the way she really would like to have done it. But every time she saw something like Doris being hit with the whips and the straps her mind also conjured up a happening in her past. But the only way such things turned her on was for masturbation. She couldn't have taken a man at such time if the Devil was stabbing her in the butt with his pitchfork. The thought at such times of being with a man and having him do things to her repulsed her...but only at such times...only then when the belts and whips and the straps were used. Any other time it was go everything all the way, take the cock deep, suck the pussy dry...but when the whips and the belts and the straps and the chains and all the other implements come out, then she can only think of masturbation...one attack at masturbation after another until the other ordeal was finished.

———

SHE WAS VERY LITTLE, very little indeed. Five or six, she couldn't remember which, but very little, and they were very poor. Tanya's father didn't work very often and when he did it was only a day at a time. Any longer than that and he wouldn't have taken the job in the first place. And when that particular type of job came along it was a swamper in a bar, a dishwasher, a street worker, and once a house painter's assistant...he stirred the paint.

It hadn't always been that way for her father. John was his name...had gone all through high school then went on to college. For two years...then he felt that the Army was closing in on him so he shot himself through the foot. From that point on he continually went down hill. There was only one problem. He had secretly married Daisy Cannon during the middle of his second year in college. And she was knocked up...pregnant...with child...going to lay another "house ape, screaming brat, fuck-head, stinking assed kid on the doorstep of the world."

Tanya hadn't heard those words then but she had heard them over and over again coming through the thin walls between her room and her father and mother's room. But it also wasn't only her room. She had four more brothers and five more sisters. Ten kids in all. And what she did remember during that fifth or sixth year was a more direct reference to her mother's capabilities.

"Ten fuckin' kids. Can't you lay down on that bed and spread your legs and take a little cum without crappin' out another of them goddam brats." He had come in, as usual after one of those day-jobs and he was tanked to the gills on the cheap wine he always swilled.

Ever since he'd shot himself in the foot he'd given out the story of the terrifying wound he'd received in the war. "Damned near shot my goddamned fuckin' foot off." But Tanya felt in later years he was reprimanding himself for what he had actually done to keep out of the war. But the wine was taking its toll on her mother as well as her father. The day worker and the washer woman and the house full of brats...and the thin wall between their sex acts and the words which came through that thin wail.

"Stinkin' kids!"

"You stink more than this whole stinkin' neighborhood. You stink of shit and you stink of that cheap wine you drink and you stink of the fuckin', fuckin' whores you pick up in the gin mills."

Then the slap...a hard one, and another and another...

"Go ahead, you bastard, kill me, you prick. Hit me and make me bleed some more then you'll get another wino hard-on and you'll fuck me and you'll have eleven of the house apes around to cuss out. Why don't you herd them all out onto the streets to hustle for you and your wine. Maybe you can afford a bigger jug next time. Take Tanya out. She's the oldest of the lot. Or would you like to fuck her too...your own kid...why don't you pick her up by the legs and bring her right up to where you are and you can stab it right down in her?"

The slapping started all over again.

"You ain't going to put me to sleep that way you bastard. You can beat me all night and all you're going to do is end up stickin' that fat, ugly prick into me. You're trouble, John, and if I had any guts about me I'd get out of here and leave you and all them brats you made me have behind. wouldn't even have to pack nothin' cause there ain't nothin' to pack. So there they are, my legs are open. Jam that prick rod home and see what you can make me poop out this time. Maybe even a black one. You had enough of the black women down at that saloon. Fuck you, you bastard! You hit me again and I'll hit a iron frying pan right over your thick skull. That's something I know will stop you."

Then there was the slapping and the punches and the kicks and the falling on the old wooden floor and the squeaking of the bed with the weight of the woman hitting it and bouncing right back up again only to be knocked right back down upon it again. Then there was a moment of silent pause until the toilet flushed and the cold water tap was turned on full blast. There was no hot water in the cold water flat.

"Shit," the woman finally screamed when the water was turned off. "You hit better than that last week, You losing your punch. Maybe someday I'll be able to get my licks in. And when I do. When I do...you ain't going to be able to piss it out in no toilet and you ain't gonna be able to wash the blood off in no sink like I do. You're only going to find the undertaker and him cuttin' them long cuts in them places just below your shoulders so he can let the blood run down the sink so's he can put that embalming fluid all up and down your body. Maybe they do flush somethin' after that, but you won't be hearing it. They say the brain is the last thing to die in the body...that's what I read once back in the college library. I only hope yours stays alive long enough to see how they cut you up and what they do before they put you in the grave."

Another slap! A quick one. But a hard one!

Then his voice. "Stretch out and open your legs." It was a demand.

"Just like always. "

"Goddamn bitch. Just like always." There was the sound of a gallon jug being slammed onto a wobbly wooden night stand. Tanya knew right where it was.

Tanya turned to look around at her sleeping brothers and sisters and wondered how they could sleep so soundly when all the world was exploding around them. Tanya couldn't know that most of the others, the older ones had heard the same thing so many times before...they were immune to words...sleep was so much more peaceful, forgiving, tranquilizing.

Tanya turned her ear to the wail again.

"God damned holey panties. You always got holes in your panties...holes in everything."

"Not in my head." Then she shouted. "Wait, don't let that be my voice speaking. I've got holes in my head forever staying with a shit piece of a bastard like you. You said it right this time buster bastard, everything around here's got holes in it. Even me."

"You got a glory hole Daisy."

"And I should use it where it does some good."

"Like out on the street?"

"You do it out there and you give it away. Maybe I could charge a little for it. At least I wouldn't have holes in my panties any more and you've sure broke my pussy hole open wide enough to take anything...even a bank roll."

One quick slap.

"Go fuck your black people. Or is it a Jap this time around?"

"Stick it up your ass."

"You tried that before and you didn't like the shit that came out with your dick. I don't know why you don't like the smell of the kids and the shit in their drawers because I can't get them changed fast enough to suit you, you smell like shit and puke every time you come into the house. You know what I do every time you cum...you fuck me and cum, then fall asleep? I'll tell you what I do. I go in the bathroom and puke and I...try to douche out. You know what I use to douche...because I ain't got the money for the proper drug store kind of stuff. I use 7-Up. I read that in one of them school books too. Health and Hygiene it was. 7-Up, you shake it up good and jam it right up the old pussy and it takes care of everything. You ever hear that. That's why I got a good smellin' pussy, and you got a sick cock...and you can only get stinkin' brats from a stinkin' cock."

There was no slap or hit then, but Tanya shuddered, she was so small and so mentally deficient about anything called life, let alone sex. But something was instilling itself within her infantile mind.

"But you still like to fuck me." It was her father's voice again, and it wasn't a tender delivery. "Come down here you big ape." And her voice was full of passion, breathy, demanding in the lowness.

"God damn, Daisy, you got a good cunt. Drunk or sober I get...you got the best cunt of anybody I ever fucked."

Then it was her hand which slapped him, time and time again across the face. The sounds were so much different than his heavy hand hitting the softer flesh.

"Now why in hell did you do that."

"Because you and your nigger fuckin'."

"Them's good ones."

"You went to college two years and you talk like a street bum."

"And you used the library, you bitch, and still talk like a whore. "

"I was a whore when you picked me up on the campus street and I'll still be a whore no matter what I read or you say. I only kept back because of you."

"You never kept back."

Tanya was to hear the same dialogue over and over again all the time she remained in that house...which was not to be much longer.

"You fucked me the first night..."

"The first half hour, then all night."

"And Tanya came along."

"Shit yes, I pooped Tanya out. She came right

through the lips of the same cunt you put your cock into and juiced all over my cunt hairs."

"I gotta have it again."

"You always gotta' have it again."

"Like you like me to beat hell outta you."

"I don't like that at all."

"You like my cock."

"I hate your stinkin' breath."

"You hate everything about me except my cock."

"You hate everything about me except my pussy."

"I hated you from the first minute I fucked you in that bar, and I hated you even worse when you told me you was knocked up...and I hated you every time from then on when you told me you was knocked up. Why can't a woman have a good fuck and not get all knocked up. What the hell is that little cum. I put it down the toilet, that. cum, why don't it make the toilet knocked up?"

"It makes maggots in the shit pot."

"I put it on the ground when I was a kid, does it grow the grass or the flowers?"

"You ever have any poison ivy or stink weed around the house. That it brings up."

"Then open that cunt...spread them legs apart 'cause Daddy's come home...and stop bleedin' all over the sheets and give me that cunt."

"What sheets?"

"Then the mattress."

"You mean the mattress you cum all over all these years."

"All you got to do is wash it when I'm away at work'"

"Work! The only work you do is to get a hard-on, lift another jug and fuck me."

"And the only work you do is poop out another kid. Why don't you use that 7-Up bottle better. Get the cum cut of you before it gets to working."

"Fuck me."

"I am."

"You ain't doing good."

"Shut up bitch. Let me concentrate."

"That really hurt me tonight John. Tomorrow I'll probably kill you."

Tanya turned her face from the thin wall and she found her finger playing with the little pea-shaped object just above the lips of her cunt and for the few minutes of excitement she heard nothing but saw the illusions of colors and sounds which seemed to take her out of reality and put her onto some kind of a pink cloud...a pink she had never seen except for the time she looked into a mirror and spread the lips of her cunt apart and there was that kind of a pink there...it was all wet...sometimes slimy...but when she diddled there with her finger she could see that same kind of pink without looking in a mirror to that spot below.

Then she seemed to explode within herself...and...

Her mother didn't live the night through. There was the slapping and the cursing, and the cunt tearing, and then she said one simple line, "I'll tear that cock and those balls out by the root."

And the next day they were taking her from that cold water flat along with the other kids and they were taking the two black rubber-covered stretchers first...the stretchers were going to the morgue and the kids were going to juvenile hall.

John had taken on Daisy, his black woman, for the last time...and she took a razor to him while she was in the death throes of a lung stab.

"I DIDN'T THINK something like this was going to happen until after we met Madam Heles," replied Danny as Tanya flipped the black lace-trimmed, red shortie negligee around her legs and moved to sit beside him on the bed. "You said it was to be midnight."

Tanya coiled her hands into the upside-down prayer form again before she spoke. "There are always preparations before Madam Heles makes her entrance...her appearance."

Danny blinked and wet his tongue and held his sopping dick in both hands. He didn't need to use both hands, he could have held the limp snake with one finger. "This is all very confusing."

Tanya shook her head sadly. She looked at the limp dick, touched it, then spread several of the fingers which had touched it across and through the hairs of her pussy.

Her eyes looked up to him and they were pleading. For the first time in her career she wasn't sure she could handle the situation of Danny Carpenter...but there was always another source. Madam Heles' establishment always had another source.

"You were confused before you came here. Soon you will not be confused any longer." It was a simple statement.

13

TANYA TURNED from Danny and crossed the room to a large, colorful tapestry. She paused in front of it, then turned her head slightly to look back to Danny. "Come! I will show you something of interest."

Danny tossed the cat-o' nine-tails, which he had been holding all this time, to the bed, then crossed to her. He looked to the tapestry curiously as her hand took an edge of it.

"Not all react to the treatments successfully. There are those who will never find a satisfaction in their... their universal language."

"What in hell is this universal language?"

Tanya pulled the tapestry aside. "Sex!"

They were then looking through a one-way glass which looked down into a massive room in which many naked men and women were in the deep throes of a sex orgy. There was no form of sexual deviation which was not being practiced...and all which were not participating at that moment wandered around the room aimlessly, restoring their vitality and recharging their batteries. Food and water were in abundance at one end of the room. But the only food and drink any of the people participated in was that given by the body and sex. They licked each other, sucked, fucked. They bit and scratched. There were the whips and the cat and the belts and the chains. There was the hair-fetishist and the fur. There were the voyeurs and the homosexuals and the lesbians. There were the drag queens dressed in the sheerest fur trimmed nighties beating their meat in well lighted corners and in front of mirrors. The same values fell upon certain women as they masturbated with dildos, fingers and whatever phallic symbol they preferred. There were love-objects of every description.

Danny felt he was looking down into a snake pit of humans who had lost all contact with life except pleasing themselves through a horror of mentally disturbed lust. Nothing was sacred to any of them. The one thought, the uppermost thought was sex in any variation. All was one and one was all of them. There was no permanent partner. Their bodies entwined with each other, clawing and twisting, snaking over one another. Few were off the fur covered floors. Their bodies wiggled and cried out in the despair of unsatisfied sexual releases. For indeed no matter how much they demanded there was always yet another, further demand. Insatiable desires ran rampant.

"Sex," replied Tanya. "Sex!" she repeated. "Some want too much...others too little. They can never return to a world which will reject them. They are happy here. And the families which originally sent them here are most overjoyed to pay the price which keeps them under our roof. They are well fed. And they are doing what they want without interference. If they were to go out onto the street there would surely await them trouble and eventually a padded cell. Would they be happy there? We are doing such a service for these poor lost sex souls."

"Why are you showing me all this?"

"Perhaps it will stimulate your mind."

"Is this some kind of a threat?"

She put her hand lightly on his hand. "There are never any threats at Madam Heles' establishment. Only on the other hand...there are always possibilities of things to come."

"Now if that ain't the damndest double talk I ever heard. Close that damned curtain."

Tanya let the tapestry fall back into place. "You are not compassionate for these lost souls?"

"According to you they're not lost souls. They're doing what they want...sort of like doing what comes naturally." She smiled broadly. "Now you are getting the point." She reached down and tickled his balls and his prick shot up instantly. "Too bad that point is so quickly demonstrative."

"I told you it always has been."

She reached down and took it in her hand and gave it three quick jerks and the purple head shot jism all over her naked cunt hairs. Once more she sighed and walked across to the bed where she wiped the spew off with a towel, then picked up her red, black trimmed negligee from the bed and put it on. She tied the single bow just under her beautiful breasts.

"I'm not reacting so well, am I?"

"The whole problem is you're reacting too quickly."

"Yeah! Shit! Maybe I should tie a string round the back of the head and keep the stuff choked up."

"Your balls would explode."

"Maybe it would backfire and come out of my ass."

She looked curiously at him. "Have you ever been fucked in the ass?"

"Good shit no! I'm no queer."

"It is not only homosexuals who have the pleasures of being fucked in the ass. There are many people who like it. Would you like to see one such case?"

Danny put his hands defiantly on his hips. His eyes narrowed. "The one thing I don't need to see is a couple of queer creeps fucking each other in the ass."

"It will be a boy and a girl. Most normal, or should we say, conventional, at other times. And she is such a pretty girl. And he is such a rugged young man."

Danny thought it over then shrugged. "What have I got to lose?" he sighed.

"Your inhibitions," smiled Tanya.

She moved to the other side of the room and adjusted a small picture behind which once more was a one-way glass. "You sure got a lot of peep holes around here. Who owned this room the last time...a peeping Tom?"

"We have always found that our guests prefer to watch others doing certain acts before they themselves are willing to indulge. Watching others do things they themselves have wanted to do but have puritanic ideas about such things seems to take some of the curse from the act."

"Watching or not. Inhibitions or not. Nobody is going to fuck me in the ass."

"They are enjoying it," she said as she looked quickly through the window, then turned back to him. "Why don't you at least give yourself the pleasure of a voyeuristic act. Come and watch."

Danny had fulfilled every request Tanya had made ever since they had first met, therefore he wasn't going to change his mind now. And there was Shirley to think of. He had promised her. And she would leave him if things didn't change. There was no doubt about that. And it would be nice if they could finally get into a bed and they could complete their marriage contract.

There was that first night, the night of their marriage. She had worn a sheer blue nightie and he had worn his suntanned skin and she was so inviting and so ready and so luscious. She tried to help him as much as she could even with her own reluctance about affairs. And there she lay with her legs open and her split beaver all sparkling, pink clean and juicy and ready for his insertion. Her breasts had swelled and her breath was hot. But she had used some lush perfume which made his cock jump up and down and he did it again as he had always done it. Only with Shirley and her exotic beauty...he didn't even get to a penetration.

The head of his cock simply touched the pubic hairs and he shot all over her. It had been that way ever since. He never got between the juicy lips...Shirley never knew what it was like to feel him deep inside of her. She had also tried the cock-sucking routine...once. He had not gotten beyond the outer lips there either. It had shot all over her chin and Shirley had had to race into the bathroom to throw up.

"I tell you," he repeated himself to Tanya, "nobody is going to fuck me in the ass."

"Watch them have fun."

She had not looked at him. Her hungry eyes were looking through the one-way glass. Danny slowly moved to her, the palms of his hands sweating, his tool sticking out in front of him in an anticipation of what he might see even though his feigned mental attitude gave out with reluctant words.

He moved in close to the glass and he saw the lovely red-head strapping on a dildo, and a really rugged man, not handsome, but then again not ugly, who was just then removing his drawers.

"I thought you said they were already having fun?"'

"They are. Sometimes the anticipation is as much an enjoyment as the act itself." She put her hand down to his cock and once more he was shooting...this time all over the wall. Tanya didn't even bother to look. She simply took her hand away and put it on her own cunt. She knew she was going to become excited.

The man, naked, crossed to the bed and lay down beside the girl. He put his hand across to the dildo strapped in exactly the right position across the girl's pussy. He made like he was jerking it off from sometime. Then the girl reached down and squeezed the plastic balls of the dildo and a milk-like liquid spurted out through the nozzle opening. This made the man go ape. He rolled over and quickly took the head in his mouth. Then he cock-sucked it as he might suck a cock. And he gobbled down the juice as rapidly as she squeezed the feigned testicles.

Tanya glanced her eyes in Danny's direction. She could see the sparkle in his eyes and she watched the tip of his tongue flicking to the dry corners of his lips.

"It's real cum, you know. We store it up from the masturbators." Then she looked back through the one-way window. "Like he is doing with the thing now."

The man had taken the dildo from his mouth and was jerking it off with his left hand while his right hand masturbated his own prick. It took him a long time but when the jism spurted, it was captured in a silver cup held by the girl. It was then that the man made a full turnaround and got down on his hands and knees on the bed. The girl made sure the dildo was completely secure at the exact point of where her lips of her cunt captured the wider, rear end. It looked as if the tool really was growing from within her body. The perfect illusion which made the man scream with the joys of anticipation when he turned his head to view the sight.

The girl, on her knees moved up slowly behind the young man and permitted the head to touch the lips of his rectum. But she didn't at that moment shove it in. She held it there, tantalizing the man. He screamed for satisfaction. His hand reached back and attempted to capture the shaft so that he, himself, could shove it home. But the girl was not about to let this happen. It was more fun prolonging the torture. She'd snap it just out of reach of the hand, then when the other hand came near she'd snap it in the other direction, but always letting the synthetic head rip across his asshole. And with each rip he screamed with delight.

"Isn't she going to use some Vaseline or something on that thing? Is he going to take it dry?" whispered Danny.

"You don't have to whisper, Danny." She didn't remove her eyes from the action in the other room. "They can't possibly hear you."

"We can hear them."

"Because of the sensitive microphones all around the room. There are microphones in almost all rooms, and some closed-circuit television also...all we have to do is turn it on whenever we want. And it is only we who know where the switches are located."

Danny looked back through the window again. "Well?"

"Well what?"

"Is she going to jam that phony cock into him raw like that...no lubricants?"

"You seem to know a lot about lubricants."

"I don't know a lot about them. But I've read a little on certain subjects. I'm not entirely stupid."

"No one has ever said you were stupid...simply a little backward...in certain instances."

Danny let the remark go. His eyes were again suddenly fascinated by what he saw and heard from the other room. The girl was still playing her little game of hide and seek with the dildo and the man was spurting his cum all over the bed. The torture of expectancy had been too much for him...but there was plenty more spunk where that had come from. And the girl was going to drive it out through the head of his cock from the rear. He was going to have his rectum filled with the soft plastic. But soft as it was the first insertion was going to hurt like hell. And if she tore some of the flesh apart, that was too bad for him. But what was too bad for him was in reality a delight for him. He'd love every moment of it and cry...scream for more. His hands would tear at the coverlet under him and his knees would pound on the bed as if her stabbings was driving him mad. And in a way, they were driving him mad. Mad with exotic delights. Every time he jumped with his knees he was forcing his anus canal tighter over the tube and this drove the shaft deeper and his prostate was getting the massage of his life. Each time he felt that he was being ruptured more and that made his life worthwhile.

Danny had watched the girl and her by-play. Then he watched in almost fascinated horror as the gigantic dildo was suddenly shoved home. It was during one of her passes when she was escaping his hands. All of a sudden she changed direction in the middle of the move and the shaft sunk into the fake balls and the screams and the pounding of the man's hands became frantic.

But there was no doubt in those screams and pounding that the man was beside himself with the sexual expectations he had been waiting for. His own shaft hardened almost immediately, and all the time she pumped from behind his cock throbbed and spurted... spurted until it looked like every bit of juice in the man's body had come through the purple head. It was impossible for him to spurt any more. But he did. Over and over again he spurted the jism and all of it fell into the silver cup.

"She'll kill him."

"If she does he will go out of this mortal world with all the pleasures he demands. But...she will not kill him."

"I say, rectum hell, it'll kill him. How can you permit such things to go on?" Danny was shooting all over the front of his legs. He couldn't contain himself even though his words seemed to belie what was really fact.

"It is too bad you are wasting all that juice. We should store it up and use it to much better advantage."

"You and your God-damned cum."

"No. Yours."

14

THE GONG which resounded throughout the house seemed to shake the very rafters. Standing on the wooden floors, covered as they were with the thick fur carpets, the resounding still felt like a shocking earthquake.

Shirley was naked on the blue fur covered bed. She had been with Barb who remained in the shortie blue, see-through affair. And Barb had been kneeling over her face. Her lips were still wet with the taste of Barb. And as the sound raced through the room the effects of Shirley's tongue exploded Barb and the sensations resounded through her own body.

Barb slowly lifted her beautiful body from her student and laid down beside her. Shirley raised up on both elbows. "What was that."

It was several moments before Barb answered. In that time she reached across to some Kleenex and wiped Shirley's beautiful mouth, then leaned in and kissed her while she permitted the soggy Kleenex to drift to a waste paper basket beside the bed.

"It is time." Barb rolled away and took up Shirley's pink nylon nightie which had been on a fur covered stand beside the bed. "Perhaps you'd like to put this on."

Shirley let her hands drift down the length of her naked body. She squealed in the delight of the feeling. "I was feeling so wonderful...nude. I never appreciated my body before, it's like I have been born all over again."

Barb leaned over again and started her tongue between the lovely girl's lips, then rivered its way down the length of her front, pausing momentarily at her belly-button, then continued down to her pussy region. She took a couple of quick swipes at the honey nectar which still clung, drying, to the pubic hairs, then rolled over so that she was again looking up toward Shirley's face.

Shirley spun around so that their faces were together. Her arms clung around Barb. "Barb...I'm scared."

"Of Madam Heles?"

"Of what lies ahead."

"There is nothing to be frightened of."

"I guess I'm all on nerves."

Barb comforted the exotically beautiful girl with another open mouth kiss and the taste of the honey of their pussies was still there. "There is no reason for nerves."

"That is not easy to accept."

"You have been a most interesting pupil." Barb dabbed her lips with two fingers.

"Is that all I've been to you...a pupil...after all we've done together."

"One day soon you will return to the outside world...and there will be Danny."

Shirley, dejected, sunk back to the bed. "Ohhhh."

Barb again moved in comfortingly. "Don't worry,

Many things have changed. And many things are still to change, You will find that Danny is being well trained."

"Danny's in training?"

Barb winked. "You can bet your sweet bippy!"

Shirley came up on her elbows again. "With whom?"

"Would it matter?"

Shirley laid back down again. "I guess not."

"Then it is Tanya, and whomever she decided upon. But the training period is over. Now is the time we must visit with Madam Heles. The hour is upon us. We must go. And you must be very proud of yourself." She reached over and touched Shirley's wet pubic hairs with two of her fingers. Then she raised the fingers to her own lips, then transported them across so that they lay briefly on Shirley's. "Your honey is like none other produced in the entire world. It is well mixed and I don't think you will ever need any other guidance, except your own, at any other time in your life."

"You will be with me?"

"All the way my darling."

"I will be frightened, out in the world again."

"You will be frightened of nothing. There will be no cock, no pussy, no deviation that you will ever be frightened of again. My only regret is that you learned so quickly. I should like to have had you for some time longer." She leaned over and kissed the girl again. "I wish you could stay longer. "

Shirley raised up to a sitting position on the blue bed. "But we were to stay two days."

"I don't think that will be any longer necessary in your case my sweet. I do believe you might receive your travel orders...tonight..."

"Travel orders?"

"You will see."

Shirley put her arm around Barb's shoulders, letting the crook of her arm settle softly in Barb's hair at the base of her neck. "Perhaps I will see something else. But I will not see the love that I have found here...a love I have found for you."

Barb kissed her again. "There will be many others."

"But none like you."

"The first is always the most enjoyable. That is the way it is said. But the others...another who will take my place. Believe me. As a teacher...I am only that. Some say that one always falls in love with their psychiatrist, their doctor, their teacher. You have fallen in love with your teacher."

"Is that all it has been? Student, teacher relationship?" Barb was the old professional. She kissed the student again. "Of course not. You have been very special. And you have been an excellent taste of honey."

"Then I am no longer frightened."

"There never has been anything to be frightened of my darling."

"The casket...Madam Heles...it is all so confusing."

"Some reside in bathtubs...others in gutters and others still out on the grass under the rain and with their bare asses on the ground under a blanket of snow. Madam Heles prefers the coffin. It is her only abode. She has her own desires, her own loves, her own way of going about life. And one must marvel in her acceptance in that she has gained the one thing all of us have been trying to do all our lives. She has found out where it really is at.

"There are so many of us who go through our entire life wondering what it is all about. And then as we enter our coffin and are lowered into the ground, we are still those who wonder what it has all been about. Why did we pass this way in the first place. What was it all about? Where did we come from and where did we go. Why does a few drops of cum from a man's penis make us pregnant, and how does it go into a fetus and then become the baby which squeals and cries in its mother's arms. Why does the small amount of cum make us feel so powerful, and what really brings it on? I suppose there are doctor's reports on all the answers. But we are the type of girls who know that making that cum spurt is a delicious experience and the more powerful that experience...the better it is for all of us.

"Perhaps every one of us will go to the grave still wondering what it was all about...but at least it will have been a real fun trip."

"Your words are so comforting."

Barb laughed lightly...almost a nervous laugh. She let her fingers drift through Shirley's pussy hair, rubbing softly, up and down, sticking her finger in and out, and Shirley's mind drifted off into the kaleidoscope of colors and pink clouds she had traveled through for the past three hours. Ever since she, reluctantly, permitted Barb to put her tongue into her cleft, and after that first explosive climax...six times...she had turned around and captured Barb's own sweet box, and her honey, with her own tongue.

Shirley had not turned around easily. It had taken much coaxing...much dialogue and even then a drop of something more in her tea. But it had been a mild mental deviation. And once she had tasted the sweet nectars of Barb's cunt...there was no stopping her. She had taken Barb's pussy with all the lust that any man might have, or any lesbian with the one thought of draining the girl dry. Shirley had come out of her shell in one quick grasp of a situation whereby she felt she knew what she wanted and did everything in striving toward that target...the target, the "V" of Barb's pussy... and she belied her name. There was no barb in Barb's pussy...only the softness and the sweet juice of human honey.

"I thought women didn't shoot...like a man?" she had questioned at that time.

And Barb came on with the only answer which was appropriate. "Perhaps we don't shoot out through the lips of our cunt...but we shoot the nectar all the same."

Shirley was to be embarrassed by her next remark. "Finger licking good, huh?" Embarrassed of course, but she had to say it...and as Flip Wilson on his television show always said, "The Devil made me say that," and she had laughed, and Barb had joined in with her.

Then, at the present. "Is Madam Heles a difficult person?"

Barb grinned broadly. But it was a soft grin. "Madam Heles only does what she believes is necessary."

"You will be with me?"

Again the hand went around Shirley's shoulder. "I will always be with you. I've told you I will be with you."

This time Shirley kissed Barb. "Then I shall not be frightened any longer."

Barb took her in her arms and lifted her from the bed. They stood together locked in each others' arms. Their hot breath, perfumed breath captured each other's imagination for the moment, as it had done many times before that evening. "There has never been any reason for fright my darling, Shirley." Then she let her go and they advanced toward the door. "But now we must go. We must keep Madam Heles waiting no longer."

"Will she be kind?"

"Hasn't everything been kind...here?" Barb, opened the bedroom door and they went out.

15

HIS EARS still rung with the sound, and when the ringing stopped there was a further thumping which could remain with him for a long time to come. However he shook his head and looked to Tanya.

"Does everything around here have to be done on such a startling scale?"

Tanya grinned. "You must admit, it is effective."

"Sure!" Danny shook his head again and pounded his right ear with the palm of his right hand. "If you want to scare hell out of somebody."

Tanya reached over and tickled his balls again. Danny got hard, but she took her hand away from the instrument before it could start spurting again. "That is only to scare the devils and the inhibitions from the mortal soul."

"When did we get around to talking about souls?"

"We all have one...do we not?"

"I don't know. I've never seen one. Have you?"

Tanya spoke seriously. "I have seen many souls."

"Well now, maybe so could I. All I'd have to know is that it was you were drinking at the time."

She nodded. "We have many potions. The life of the necromancer is made up of items like potions. But there is not alcohol such as you know it from the saloons and the cocktail lounges. We are not so stupid as to destroy our liver with such disturbing influences. We have much more use for our bodies than to make them the swill receptacle of worthless crap."

"My, how you do talk."

"As I said. The sounds around Madam Heles' establishment are perfectly designed. Remember? To drive out the devils and the inhibitions."

"Why in hell do you keep harping about inhibitions. You're getting to sound like Shirley every time she refers to my manhood. The one thing I've got is plenty of manhood. And I have never known I had any inhibitions."

"Nearly all humans have some form of inhibitions. All around us, except those who successfully graduate Madam Heles' establishment of exotic pleasures."

He raised the palm of his hand to a position a foot over his head. "You know I can hear those words, Madam Heles' establishment until I think the whole structure is full of shit right up to here."

"Oh, you are a difficult one."

"From now on I mean to be."

"Oh, I think you'll change your mind." She touched his cock again...

...and he pulled sharply back. "You don't know me very well. When I make up my mind it stays made. And you can stop playing with my prick. It's not going to do you any good."

Tanya looked down to the massive hard-on. "I see that it does no good."

Danny slapped hell out of the well-used purple head

and it immediately went down. "What you can raise up, I can sure as hell knock down."

"I wonder how hard you would have to slap it if I were to put my beautiful, red lips around it. Lick it with my tongue. Let the rivers of spit, the hot saliva run all around the base of that head then up and down the shaft. I wonder how many slaps it would take then before you are shooting all over the floor once more."

"Ohh, shit."

"Shit is the final discharge of waste materials. I don't think you really know what the world thinks of shit, or you wouldn't be letting it come out of your mouth so often."

For the moment Danny didn't have a comeback. He simply, absently, wiped his lips on the back of his hand. "What was that noise?"

"A signal."

"That I figured."

"Madam Heles is ready to receive us."

"Well holy shit..."

"Shit is never joly."

"I didn't mean it that way."

"Perhaps you don't know what you mean."

"For the last half hour all you've been doing is attempting to confuse me." He waved away the words she had started to build. "Yeah, I know. I was confused before I came here. I won't be confused when I leave."

"That is quite correct."

"So where do we go from here?"

"We will return to the red room."

"Where the big bronze box is."

"Where Madam Heles holds court."

"I knew court would figure in here someplace."

"Madam Heles never leaves that room."

"You mean she can?"

"Insults will get you nowhere."

"Ahh, hell." He finally softened and a smile crossed his face. "I don't really mean to be insulting. You girls sure have given me a hell of a good time this day, and I'm grateful. I don't even know how I got it up all those times, let alone spurt off so many times."

"I do...but you will have not learned to hold it like a man...like a man who can please his lady...perhaps any lady he chooses."

"You mean like my spurting off so quickly."

She nodded.

"I still don't think there's anything I can ever do about that. I see a beautiful woman and that's all there is to it...up comes junior and pretty quick it's spurting all over the place. Let that same girl take it in her hand, touch it with her lips...and pop...off it goes and I go off into seventh Heaven. That's something which isn't going to be corrected easily...even the doctors and the psychiatrists I went to a long time ago said they couldn't help me. Shirley doesn't know about those type of medical visits I had."

"I'm sure she doesn't...and I'm equally as sure you did not tell all when you should have."

"Now you're really talking in riddles!"

"Few ever tell another what their real problem ls. Few really know it. And few will continue with the learned men until the real reason has been searched out.

"We here at Madam Heles use the couch the same as a psychiatrist...but we ask few questions. So much is poured out of the cock or the cunt which cannot come out of the mouth. The mouth is used for so much...yet it only ends up spewing out platitudes, feigned surprises, curses when there is nothing else to be said...and lies to one's own self."

"I'm not a liar."

"That is for your own conscience."

"Damn, sometimes I love you and other times I want to kill you."

"As, perhaps you did a teacher, or even your psychiatrist?"

"Shit!"

"The mouth again."

"Shhhhiiiiittttt!"

"Dragging anything out always prolongs the agony. Shall we go?"

"Where?"

"I've already told you. To the red room."

"And once there?"

"We shall know that when the time comes."

"That's the fucking irritating thing about this whole joint-"

Tanya cut in. "Establishment."

"Fucking joint. I said it and that's what I mean. JOINT." He spun back to the window where the whipping and the lashing had been going on. He threw back the small curtain. It was completely dark inside.

"What happened to them?"

"When Madam Heles summons someone to her chambers, there is no other action within the entire establishment. It is the rule."

"Honor am0ng prostitutes."

"The name prostitute has, in its time, held an esteemed place of honor."

"Don't give me another one of your historical lectures."

He let the curtain fall back into place, then turned back fully to 'Tanya. "Where's Shirley?"

"She will be waiting...for us."

"In the red room?"

"In the direct abode of Madam Heles."

"There we go again." He crossed to her and laid his hand lightly on her shoulder. "You know Tanya. You might have been a hell of an interesting broad if I had picked you up in one of my...cocktail lounges...where the alcohol is of a different nature."

"I doubt if I'd have been very interesting. In the days of my...cocktail lounge entrances."

"So now to the red room."

"To, perhaps, something more."

Danny sat down on the edge of the bed, reached over and took up the red pajama pants. He surveyed them with a glint of glee in his eye. He felt the words he was forming were a cut of some kind. He wasn't quite sure what kind of a cut, but at least they were going to be some kind of a humor to him.

"For such a fancy setting do you think these are conventional enough?"

Tanya was serious. "The word conventional can take on many connotations. Never more so than in this establishment."

The words seemed to echo in his ears as if he had heard them before. He was almost sure he had, but he couldn't figure where or when. It was like the times he was in some place and felt he had been there before but knew he hadn't...yet had he. He could describe any movement...or if a place, any tree, any house...any twig. During his youthful life he had had several visitations of a like nature. He pulled on the trousers and let the elastic waist band snap around his tight middle. There was a loud snap and he feigned sudden pain, then laughed. "Well...conventional or not...I guess here we go."

Knowingly. "Here we go."

But Danny took her hand in his. He licked at the edges of his lips with the tip of his tongue. "Madam..."

"That word is reserved for Madam Heles..." Tanya let him lead her out of the room, but once in the corridor she took over the command.

16

UPON ENTERING the red room Danny found Shirley and Barb already in attendance. Although he'd never met the lovely Barb before he could readily see that Shirley held more than a light friendship for her. There was a sparkle in her eyes which he had never seen before. Or at least not since the early days of their courtship.

He moved to stand beside Shirley and a strange look came into Barb's eyes. It might have been the start of hatred, then perhaps of jealousy, or simply irritation. However, her hand dropped down and softly took Shirley's. Then all was well again. But Danny was not to remain in that position very long. Tanya led him across the room with her and then turned so that she and Danny were facing Barb and Shirley.

"So where have you been?" he finally advanced to Shirley.

"I could ask you the same question."

Danny put his hands on his hips, He captured the silly smile he was so famous for. "I had a delightful time."

Shirley squeezed Barb's hand for reassurance, then directed her words to Tanya. "Did she?"

Tanya grinned. "When at first you don't succeed, try, try again." Barb suppressed a giggle and Danny felt tike crawling into the nearest hole.

He wanted to get out of that room. Out of that building. But apparently it was too late. He'd gone loo far, and he felt there was no turning back. He felt naked to the world even though he had on the pajama trousers. His hands crossed in front of his cock as if to hide it when it was already hidden, and nothing had excited him. It was still limp and had been ever since the last time...when Tanya had touched it. However the thought of her touching it gave the prick a slight jounce which was quite noticeable under the loose materials.

Shirley blinked and Barb giggled again. Tanya's look had been too late to see the slight action. But Danny turned as red as the pants and she knew what probably had happened. And her mind drifted quickly back to those most recent times, with him trying so vainly to keep the cum in his prick the way she had attempted to teach him. But how each time it spurted off completely out of control.

Of course she had never come across such a man before. There had been many who were quickie artists, like Karl and a few others still in the home. But at least they could stay in the saddle long enough to get a girl heated up...at least so she could finally get herself off with her finger or the use of a dildo, or even by getting tongued by another girl...she liked the girl part almost as much as she did masturbation. But she didn't consider herself as a lesbian. Perhaps a part-time lesbian, definitely double gaited. But then that was her life, she had to be prepared to take on all comers.

She did feel a bit cheated, however. She would like to have had more time with Danny. After all he was a darned good-looking guy and he was built like a bull stud. She felt quite confident that given enough time she could plug up that hole in his dam. But Madam Heles only gave a specified amount of time for any of her girls for the introductory training period. They had to be serviced and judged as to what course must be taken. If they were not in tune to the operation then the most drastic steps had to be taken.

Those drastic steps were always directed by Madam Heles. And Madam Heles was always kept informed as to the progress so that when she appeared she was ready to take whatever step was necessary.

"Well, where is this Madam Heles?" questioned the irritated voice of Danny.

"In due time."

"To hell with your due time shit."

"Oh, Danny, stop using that word." Shirley sighed and Barb held on to her hand even more tightly. She also stepped closer so that their bodies met through the sheer nightgowns.

Danny noticed the move. "You going for girls this week?"

"Barb is a real friend."

"That's her name?"

Barb grinned over her ruby red lips, sparkling, shining lips. "Perhaps, handsome, we will meet under different circumstances...later."

His cock suddenly rose up and stuck the material far out in front. He had visualized sticking it into the girl in blue. And the next thing he knew he was shooting and the dark stain swelled on the front of the red pants. He clasped his hands over the area, but there was no really hiding it.

"He should carry a towel with him at all times," grinned Barb.

"I won't stand here and be insulted."

"Nobody is insulting you," grinned Barb. "We do feel a bit sorry for you. But you are not a hopeless case."

"Shirley's been talking. She's been saying things about me."

"It matters little," said Tanya, "whether or not Shirley has said one word. Everything has been recorded. All is known. Everything must be known before we stand here in front of Madam Heles. Remember how I told you about the microphones and the closed-circuit television cameras? It is all recorded and can be played back at anytime.

"Perhaps if matters do not improve you will have to see yourself in action. Some find it quite pleasant."

Danny blushed again. "Well at least I didn't take it in the ASS."

He felt silly saying the words. But there they were floating out on the ether and there was no retracting them. He glanced across to Shirley to see how she reacted to that, but there was little expression on her face. She had learned to expect anything from him...even more since they had entered the establishment and she had seen so much of sex which she had never dreamed existed.

She had been pampered and loved, and that was something she had always needed. She had never had any real love with her mother and father. Real love couldn't come from such an environment. Real love couldn't ever come through the strictness of the rod and the staff or from religious words which meant nothing.

She had never learned anything in her parents' home, which could be adjudged appliable to the outside world.

She had been left on her own to find out what was necessary all by herself, and up until that time and the meeting with Barb, she had learned very little. She had been so unsatisfied by Danny. How many nights had she cried herself to sleep, not even bothering to use her finger on herself. It was against all she had ever been taught. She could grow hair on the palm of her hands... she would go insane from masturbating.

But there was one thing which even her mind couldn't stop, and that was her wet dreams. There had been times when she visioned up all sorts of sexual delights and somehow she found herself climaxing.

For more months than she cared to remember, it had been the only way she had ever gotten any measure of release. But there had to be more to sex than feigned illusions.

She knew what a man was and what he was supposed to do and how she was supposed to feel. She remembered the father of her child and even through the pain there had been some great feeling which surged through her body, but the fear of detection and the fear of God held back even the full enjoyment of that situation.

She wondered where her child was and who the mother and the father were. She could never see the child again and that really didn't bother her too much.

But to have had that child through all the pain and still to never have experienced any of the joys which were supposed to be connected with the affair...that was almost more than she could bear.

Danny had seemed like the right guy. They had never done anything before they acquired the marriage license and faced the preacher. In fact they had never done anything anyway. She had never known what a climax was until those recent few hours with Barb. There was no doubt but what Barb had turned her on to the heights she never realized existed. And in so thinking she squeezed Barb's hand and the girl knew what the thoughts were.

But Shirley also knew that woman love was not going to be the complete answer. All it had proved to her was that she could climax and that it was an enjoyable feeling. And she knew she wanted to feel what it was like with a man. She had all the normal reactions to that particular type of thought. And she let her eyes drop to the slight bulge in the front of Danny's pajama pants, and the stain which was quickly drying and she shivered all over.

Barb put her arm tenderly around the girl's waist and hugged her briefly. Then as Tanya turned to the altar and the coffin, Barb let go of the girl and moved to kneel with Tanya. They both looked to the coffin and there was a moment as if in silent prayer.

Then both girls turned to each other and they embraced tightly, their lips cementing together and, through the movements of their cheeks it was apparent that their tongues were smashing together, and their stifled cries told that their sexual fires were being kindled.

Their hands drifted downward. Tanya's found the beautiful globes of Barb's tittles through the sheer blue baby-doll nightie. Barb's own hand drifted down and played openhanded with Tanya's cunt. It played there a long time before the long finger was inserted.

Tanya moaned with delight and she suddenly bent far back and opened her legs wide, although she retained the kneeling position. Then in one wild, almost terrifying scream, she released all the sex energy which had suddenly built within her.

Then after several quivering retakes of the same sensations, she bent forward and buried her face deep into Barb's crotch. She gobbled hurriedly and Barb bent her head back in the ecstasy of the moment. She made cooing sounds which sounded much like the noises pigeons make when they are startled. But there was no doubt that Tanya's tongue was searing her delightful honey box.

Danny crossed to Shirley. "Maybe I got problems... but I'd sure hate to have the ones they got."

Shirley sighed. "What's the matter? Couldn't you handle it again?"

"Good God, the people around here could kill you. They've about got me milked dry."

"Is that why there's a stain on the front of your pants." She eyed him coldly then turned to watch the girls make love in front of the altar.

"Damn. That's weird," Danny muttered, but his hand was holding his stiff cock through the pajama pants.

Shirley saw the bulge and inadvertently let her hand drop to it. She encircled the shaft, through the nylon material, just behind the head and the sticky fluid seeped through the nylon and covered her hand. She pulled the hand away and wiped it on the side of his pajama covered leg.

"Yep," she sighed. "The same old Danny."

"Shhhhiiiittttt..." he muttered, then crossed back to the position where Tanya had left him.

Barb didn't scream as she cum off. But she closed her eyes and held her breath until her face turned almost as blue as her nightie. Then she exploded time and time again. Her hips jammed up into Tanya's face and Tanya met each lunge with a downward motion.

Then the last of the eruptions dwindled and both girls stood up. Barb returned to Shirley and kissed her hungrily on the lips. Danny might have said something but he was immediately confronted by Tanya who put her arms around him.

"Taste Barb's honey. It is most delightful."

She clamped her lips over his and forced her sticky tongue through his lips and he was swallowing the other girl's juices. And it was sweet. "That is one of the sweetest cunts you will ever taste. Is it any wonder she has captured Shirley's mind?"

"Captured Shirley's...she and Shirley?"

"Does that shock you."

"But Shirley...Shirley doesn't know how to do anything. Nothing at all."

Barb grinned. "You have so many surprises in store for you. So many surprises indeed."

"Hey...what's been going on behind my back?"

Tanya tipped a finger to his lips. "Nothing more than what has been going on with you."

"Hell's fire. I wasn't with any man."

Tanya grinned. "Neither was Shirley."

"Ohh, come on," he fired. "You gotta be kidding. This is all got to be some kind of a nightmare. This can't really be happening. I know I'm going to hear some kind of a sound which is going to wake me right up and I'll see the daylight again. This has got to be nuts."

"We are here to assure you that all is well. You are in no dream. And you have never cum so many times in your life. Now isn't that proof of our reality?"

"One thing for sure. I guess I never have cum like I cum around here. That's a fact."

"Take all the joys you can from this life," said Barb slowly, again putting her arm around the pink-clad Shirley. "There are so few joys on the outside world. We are here for only that one purpose. To give joys in the only way we know how...and in the only way where thorough enjoyment may come to the human being... may come to all the inhabitants of the earth.

"Sexual joys are the most important, motivating force in all the world...all the universe. You must learn to love sex in all its forms. The only reason one is powerless in gratifying themselves and their partner is because they are ignorant about sex itself. When one is ignorant as to positions and deviations there is no doubt but what they must go through life unfulfilled. When sex is properly handled, and properly digested life becomes a real thing where little can come to boredom.

"We are here to teach all the paths through the sexual forests. And if sometimes we must stop and drink of life's nectar then it is only to restore vigor to the body. We must stop often to drink of that honey. Sex must never have any boundaries. It must be free for all to enjoy. There must be no restraints. Sexual freedom should be the first aim of the world. With such a sexual freedom there then can come only happiness.

"Think of the wars and we then think of unhappiness. Would it not be better if all those men were in bed with some woman...or with themselves for that matter? There would be no time for wars in such a case. There would only be time to cum and to cum over and over again. Think of all the emotions which would flow through that enjoyable sensation while you cum and cum over and over again. A never-ending tide of sensual delights.

"Shirley has felt the sensual delights for the first

time. It will not be her last. It will not be her last because she has had the experience and will want to live it over and over again. She will never be drawn back into that sexually starved hulk of a woman which she has previously been."

Tanya faced him directly. "And because of that you must learn what it takes to please her. And it is not in the way you have been doing things. You must learn to hold back, to give her all the thrill that your giant shaft can give her. It has not been Shirley who has been the problem Danny Carpenter, but you your-self. No woman can please the man she loves if he cannot please her.

"This is not a world any longer where the woman is just a plaything for the male. She is not simply a receptacle of his cum juices...laying there to give the man his jolly joys he can go off about his business. She MUST be pleased, then she can return that pleasure a thousandfold.

"You have been the problem all along."

Then there was the weird moaning from inside the coffin. Danny nervously snapped to it. Shirley was held from any kind of fright by the comforting hand of Barb. Then Tanya slowly turned to face the bronze box.

"We await your appearance oh, Madam Heles."

The moaning seemed to become more strong...then it faded, then returned.

"We are all in attendance, Madam Heles," said the prayer-like voice of Barb as she mirrored some of the words Tanya had first spoken.

"I come..." told the moaning words.

Then the coffin lid slowly creaked open. One might not expect such creaking from such a polished box, nor would one expect the sound of thunder racing across a mountain path, but the thunder was there and the sounds of a heavy wind...and the figure which rose up from the depths of the purple, velvet-lined box might have been beautiful, but it was impossible to really tell through all the heavy make-up. But the lips were shiny and blood red, and the teeth, white, sharp and long.

Her fingers were talons with blood red nails, and the arms were soft, but there didn't appear to be any meat under the fleshy skin. However her naked breasts were a delight to behold through the sheer black shroud which was casually draped over her head and shoulders.

Madam Heles might have been dead and she might have been alive. It was hard to really be sure. Danny was immediately impressed with the thought that she was really dead. She was moving, and her pink tongue caressed the red lips. But she had to be the dead revisiting.

Then the thunder died away into the distance and the loud wind became a simple whisper. The startling, ebony black eyes of Madam Heles surveyed the small group.

There was no attempt at a welcome of any kind. She simply let her gaze stop on Shirley for a long moment, then traversed across to Danny.

"Your report," said the hollow voice and both Danny and Shirley shivered at the sound, "is well understood."

"It is thorough, Madam Heles." Tanya cupped her hands downward in the prayer form she always used.

"I am sure it is. And what are the final thoughts to disposition?" Danny felt another cold shiver capture his body as the further words came from the ghoul.

Barb stepped forward with Shirley. She held on to her hand tightly. "This is Shirley."

"Yes..." The eyes narrowed approvingly. "She is a delightful looking piece."

"Most delightful," replied Barb.

"And she has fared well?"

"It was never her fault in any affair. We have come to that conclusion. She has proved exceptional in her acceptance of all which has been taught her. She will enjoy her stay with us...and she will learn many of the routines which have so long been held from her. And she will learn beautifully. And when she returns to the world she will no longer have any sexual fears...which will release her mind to the acceptance of life for what it is and she will accept the untold joys which await her new spirit."

The necromancer made a pass, slowly, with her arm and the talon fingers showed even more than before. But there was tremendous authority through the passing of that arm through the air. And the authority held in her voice. "Then she may pass henceforth into an entity for the world of sex. For all time she shall know what sex is and how to enjoy it." She then was silent and fastened those black eyes on the girl.

Shirley blinked. She looked to Barb. "What happens now, Barb?"

Barb grinned. "You've graduated."

Shirley smiled.

Barb held her grin. "You will now have a wonderful stay here with us."

Danny slammed his hands to his hips. "Hey, what about me?" Fire started to steam through his eyes.

Tanya eyed him coldly, "There are more corrective measures which must be dealt you. But when you leave you will be a credit to Shirley...that I can promise you."

The witch turned her eyes fully on Danny. "He has not com across."

"He's cum across too many times, too quickly."

"I see."

Tanya continued. She looked from him to the coffin. She made the thumbs down movement. "No feeling! No nothing. Completely void of sexual stimulation acceptance. Speed in ejaculation has been apparently his goal throughout his entire life. Whether he has ever known it or not he has never had any feeling for his love partner. l believe this to be an opinionated motive stemming from something in his extreme youth."

"Hey now wait a minute. You can't talk about me like I wasn't here."

"He talks, but he does not listen," scowled the necromancer.

"As he does with his sex life. His partner's urges cry out for satisfaction, but his own sexual urges do not respond or listen. They are completely selfish in passing from his loin and into the receptacle.

Shirley developed troubled eyes. She leaned in close to Barb and whispered. "What will they do to him?"

"He will go into severe training."

"They won't hurt him."

"It is all according to how strong his mind is, and how he can accept the inevitable."

"Please don't hurt him."

"You do love him so much."

"Yes...very much. I could never love any other man. But if only he could..."

"Hold back the flood. Why don't you stop your fretting and I'm sure everything will turn out alright for both of you." She put the comforting pressure into her hand again. "All will be well...I assure you."

The woman in the coffin reached to the front opening of her sheer black shroud and brought out her right tit which she laid over the edge of the coffin. Her black eyes suddenly sparkled in anticipation. She licked the corners of her blood red lips with the end of her wet, pink tongue. She crooked a finger at Danny.

"Then he needs the personal services of Madam Heles."

"That is our combined thought Madam Heles," said Tanya and bowed with respect.

"It shall be done."

Tanya stepped back, but to a position very close to Danny. She had not, however, taken her eyes from the woman in the coffin. "Deliverance is at hand."

"So shall it be." The necromancer looked again to Shirley. "For one so true, she should have the love of the right man. And if the right man is this one, then the drastic measures must be taken. They will have a delightful time in the establishment of Madam Heles."

She suddenly reached up both hands and made one single sharp clap.

Two robust men shot into the room and grabbed Danny's both arms. Tanya reached in and ripped the red nylon pajama trousers from his body.

"Hey...what in hell's going on here? What are you doing to me?"

His cries raised to panic proportions as the men forced him across the room and to the coffin as Madam Heles ran back down. His cries became even more frantic as they lifted him and stuffed him into the coffin with the corpse-like occupant. "No...no...for God's sake don't! I'll freak. Don't put me in that thing. I'll freak out...I'll go mad." The talon fingers drifted up through his hair and he was forced down upon the full breasts.

With all the terror in him he still couldn't help but get a hard on. But he didn't apparently notice that. The bony arms held him firm and brought his screaming lips down over her blood red ones and the two men lowered the lid of the coffin and locked it over his already stifled screams. And when the lid was firmly locked there was only the muffled cries which sounded as if they came from a long way off. Shirley looked from girl to girl through her wide eyes. Barb however put a comforting hand on her arm and smiled to comfort her that all would be alright.

Then the cries became sobs...then the sobs became moans...then moans of pleasure...then cries of delight...then of pure joy from within the box and Danny was suddenly heard to shout from that long distance off.

"Good God...good God. She's done it. By God she's done it...I'm a man. I'm a man...I'm finally a man who can please a girl...I'm really a man at last!"

THE END

about the author

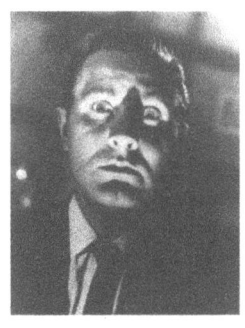

Edward Davis Wood Jr. was a filmmaker, actor, and author from America who garnered notoriety for the campy aesthetics, technical errors, unsophisticated special effects, ill-fitting stock footage, eccentric casts, idiosyncratic stories, and non sequitur dialogue in his films. He was largely unknown until he posthumously received a Golden Turkey Award for Worst Director of All Time in 1980. Afterwards, his movies became the subject of renewed public interest. A New York native, Wood developed interests in performing arts and pulp fiction quite early in his life. In the 1950s, Wood directed numerous low-budget science fiction, crime and horror films. In the 1960s and 1970s, he started making sexploitation and pornographic films. He authored more than 80 pulp fiction crime, horror, and sex novels. After Rudolph Grey's oral biography 'Nightmare of Ecstasy: The Life and Art of Edward D. Wood Jr' was published in 1992, a biopic on his life, titled 'Ed Wood', was made by Tim Burton, with Johnny Depp portraying Wood. The film earned two Academy Awards.

www.ingramcontent.com/pod-product-compliance
Lightning Source LLC
Chambersburg PA
CBHW010934120626
46552CB00010B/3252